I'm a monster and I'm im
fear. As heir to my father's
but my secret desires may keep me from fulfilling those
expectations.

One night, a stranger kisses me. In his touch, I see the
possibility of a life beyond my prison. My name? Just call
me Angel and this is my evolution.

MLR Press Authors

Featuring a roll call of some of the best writers of gay erotica and mysteries today!

Derek Adams	Z. Allora	Maura Anderson
Simone Anderson	Victor J. Banis	Laura Baumbach
Helen Beattie	Ally Blue	J.P. Bowie
Barry Brennessel	Nowell Briscoe	Jade Buchanan
James Buchanan	TA Chase	Charlie Cochrane
Karenna Colcroft	William Cooper	Michael G. Cornelius
Jamie Craig	Ethan Day	Diana DeRicci
Vivien Dean	Taylor V. Donovan	Theo Fenraven
S.J. Frost	Kimberly Gardner	Michael Gouda
Kaje Harper	Alex Ironrod	AC Katt
Thomas Kearnes	Sasha Keegan	Kiernan Kelly
K-lee Klein	Geoffrey Knight	Christopher Koehler
Matthew Lang	J.L. Langley	Vincent Lardo
Anna Lee	Elizabeth Lister	Clare London
William Maltese	Z.A. Maxfield	Timothy McGivney
Tere Michaels	AKM Miles	Reiko Morgan
Jet Mykles	William Neale	N.J. Nielsen
Cherie Noel	Willa Okati	Erica Pike
Neil S. Plakcy	Rick R. Reed	A.M. Riley
AJ Rose	Rob Rosen	George Seaton
Riley Shane	Jardonn Smith	DH Starr
Richard Stevenson	Liz Strange	Marshall Thornton
Lex Valentine	Haley Walsh	Mia Watts
Missy Welsh	Stevie Woods	Ian Young
Lance Zarimba	Mark Zubro	

Check out titles, both available and forthcoming, at
www.mlrpress.com

Angel's Evolution

Transformation Series Book One

T.A. Chase

mlrpress
www.mlrpress.com

This book is a work of fiction. Names, characters, places, and incidents either are products of the author's imagination or are used fictitiously. Any resemblance to actual events or locales or persons, living or dead, is entirely coincidental.

Copyright 2012 by T.A. Chase

All rights reserved, including the right of reproduction in whole or in part in any form.

Published by
MLR Press, LLC
3052 Gaines Waterport Rd.
Albion, NY 14411

Visit ManLoveRomance Press, LLC on the Internet:
www.mlrpress.com

Cover Art by Deana Jamroz
Editing by Kris Jacen

Print ISBN# 978-1-60820-723-7
Ebook ISBN#978-1-60820-724-4

Issued 2012

This book is licensed to the original purchaser only. Duplication or distribution via any means is illegal and a violation of International Copyright Law, subject to criminal prosecution and upon conviction, fines and/or imprisonment. This eBook cannot be legally loaned or given to others. No part of this eBook can be shared or reproduced without the express permission of the publisher.

The Beginning

The first ball of the Season and I'm in pain. I can't move without the fabric of my shirt scraping against the welts on my back. My coat is black velvet, so should any blood leak through, no one can tell. I slide over to stand behind a large potted palm. I don't know anyone here and doubt anyone would make an effort to come and talk to me.

I'm used to being invisible. Father ignores me unless he's angry. Then I'm his whipping boy. I stare down at the bruise circling my wrist. He'd dragged me out of my room and forced me to get dressed. He says I need to go around in Society. Maybe the Ton will rub off on me. I shiver as a piercing laugh rings over the music. There is no way I want to be a part of them. They are cold like my father and that scares me.

I edge closer to the door leading out into the garden. The air is getting heavy. I'm having a hard time breathing. I pant, trying not to panic or faint. Father wouldn't approve of me making a scene. Someone brushes against my arm and I murmur an apology. I don't make eye contact. My father has taught me the folly of showing any type of defiance.

As I make my escape into the night, someone runs into my back and I bite my lip to keep from crying out. Pain causes tears to swim in my eyes. I rush down the path to where I can hide without anyone noticing me. I throw my head back and fight the tears while I glare up at the moon. Silver light bathes my face. I long to be away from here. I will never fit in.

My differences are more than just my shyness. My father says I have the devil inside. He claims my secret longings are the path leading me to Hell. I don't know how he knows about them. He has yet to understand that he makes my life hell, so maybe finally following that path would ease the pain.

A noise draws my attention. Looking back at the veranda and the doors leading into the ballroom, I see a silhouette. It's a man. He stands, staring out into the darkness as if he is searching for something or someone. I shrink farther into the shadows of the bushes. I know he isn't searching for me, but I won't risk getting caught and pulled back into that room.

The man stays outside for a few minutes. I don't move. He turns and heads through the doors. Before he disappears into the swirling kaleidoscope of the ball, he looks back. I stumble as I step back. It feels as if his gaze touches me. Yet he can't know that I'm out here. As he melts into the crowd, I see the glint of gold as the light hits his hair.

§ § § §

One night later...

I'm not in as much pain tonight. I managed to avoid incurring Father's wrath last night. So he has had no reason to beat me, though that has never stopped him before. I mingle with the people, but don't stop to say anything to anyone. I don't know what they are talking about. I'm isolated in my father's home and gossip doesn't reach my ears. The servants don't even talk to me.

I make my way over to the punch. I'm dipping out a glass when a woman stops next to me.

"Hello."

I glance around me to make sure she's talking to me. Shock rushes through my body. *Why would she wish to talk to me?* My hand shakes. I'd fear a trap by my father, yet I know he isn't in the room to watch me make a fool of myself. When I look at her, she's staring at me with expectant eyes.

Taking a deep breath, I say, "Hello."

She laughs softly. "I was afraid you would ignore me. Nothing worse than being ignored by a handsome man."

Heat fills my cheeks. Handsome? I wonder if she is blind. I'm not handsome. My father tells me that every day. Not knowing what to do, I hand her my glass of punch. She takes it and thanks me.

"I know it's not proper for us to talk to each other without being introduced." She laughs. "I've never been accused of being particularly proper. My name is Alice." She holds out her free hand.

I rub mine on my thighs and bow over hers. I stutter over my name. I have no real connection to my name. It's my father's and therefore I have no claim to it.

Her kind green eyes smile at me and I don't feel like such a fool. Alice isn't beautiful like many of the ladies I see circling the dance floor, but there is a beauty in her face that tells me she is a gentle soul. She looks out into the crowd and nods.

"It's nice to meet you, Lord Robert. Unfortunately, I'm being summoned. Maybe we will meet again soon." She brushes her hand over my arm and disappears into the mob of people.

I dip out another glass of punch for myself. As I turn to face the dance floor, someone bumps into me. The jostling isn't hard enough for me to spill my drink, but still I know someone has run into me. An intriguing scent of whiskey and man drifts into my nose. It is a scent I've smelled before, though I can't remember where. Something about it causes my body to tense and the oddest sensation courses to my groin, making my prick hard.

I abruptly set my glass down and move away. Feeling that way is wrong. I've learned that punishment comes after the rising of my manhood. I wind around the room to find shelter behind another potted plant. I'll stay here until Father is ready to go. Maybe I can avoid the whip tonight.

§ § § §

The next night...

I wander out on the veranda, escaping the crush of people and perfume. I stroll to where the rail meets the wall and creates a small alcove to hide in. Shadows cover me as I stare out into the garden.

Couples are slipping off farther down the paths. Some part of me wonders what they do in the darkness, away from prying eyes. I have no experience with the opposite sex, not that I want any. I've found to my pain that my interest lies in another direction.

A boot scuffing the stone steps catches my attention and I shrink closer to the wall, praying that the ivy will hide me.

A man stands just outside the doors. He stares out over the garden and sighs. If I were anyone else, I would ask him why he sighs with such melancholy. Instead I pray he doesn't see me.

A gentle breeze blows towards me. I catch the scent of whiskey and man. My body tenses and I press farther into the shadows. This aroma has caught my attention before, but always in the midst of a crowd in a ballroom. My eyes strain to see the face of this elusive man.

Another man joins him on the veranda and I bite my lip to keep from whimpering. I can't be seen. If my father knew I snuck away from the ball, he'd punish me.

"Why are you out here instead of fending off the ambitious mothers back in there?" The newcomer gestures back to the house.

"I can't think while I'm in there, Harry. There's too much noise and it's far too hot for me." The first man looks up into the night sky.

"Thinking? What's bothering you that you need to run away to think about it?" Harry glances over his shoulder. "You can't spend too much time out here. Someone will come and drag you back in soon."

"An angel, Harry. I'm thinking about an angel." The longing in the man's voice brings tears to my eyes.

"Do you really think one exists?" Harry squeezes the man's shoulder.

"You found yours. My angel eludes me at every turn. But some day, I'll be able to hold mine. I know it." He glances up at the stars once more and turns to face the ballroom. "Let's go back in. I have no wish to be dragged back by some simpering maid."

I edge from my hiding place as they walk through the door. I want to look at this man who longs for an angel. The light bathes his blond hair, turning it to glistening gold. He's tall and masculine, dressed in black. He turns as if he knows I'm watching. Our eyes meet. His brilliant sky blue eyes light up with joy. He takes a step towards me and I whirl around, running from the veranda and into the dark garden.

I know I'm being foolish. The joy in his eyes is not for me. He must have seen another friend or a lady he loves. I can't control the shivers racing down my spine. It would be my ultimate dream to have a man such as him look at me with that much joy in his face.

I drop to my knees, retching as fear tangles in my heart. My back begins to ache. I can't think those thoughts. Father would chain me in my room for days if he knew I'd grown hard at the sight of that stranger. My father calls me a monster and I think he's right. For only a possessed man would wish for the touch of another man.

Yet a voice deep from my soul tells me that love is the most precious thing in the world. It doesn't matter who the lovers are as long as they love. It's hard to believe that when the wounds on my back begin to throb.

I climb to my feet, shaking with fear and despair. Love is not for me. I'm chained to this dark world and haven't the courage to break the links holding me down. An image of a golden god with blue eyes flashes through my mind and I know I'll always have a secret fantasy of someone loving me, no matter who or what I am.

REBIRTH

Part One

One week later...

I stand in the shadows of the ballroom. Beautiful men and women whirl by me but I only see them as flashes of color on the edge of my vision. Like a moth drawn to a flame, my eyes focus on him. My cheeks flush and I feel myself stiffen. I step farther back into the dark, hiding from the society I was born a part of. I have been watching him since he arrived an hour ago. The others defer to him and the very way he carries himself tells me he's an important man. I wonder what his name is. He is the man I saw standing on the veranda a week ago. The man who's looking for an angel.

Flashing a smile, he brushes a kiss over the knuckles of a simpering lady. His golden hair glistens under the candlelight and my fingers itch to run through his curls. Shame burns through me. I understand that my longings aren't normal. If anyone knew about them, I'd be scorned. My father has taught me the pain of being different. I pause in my admiration of the blond man to wonder why my father has brought me to London for the Season. It certainly can't be to find a wife for I fear that will never happen.

Women leave me cold. I appreciate their beauty, but have no urge to lie with them. They are too soft. I fear hurting them in my passion. Chances have been given to me to enjoy the pleasures of a woman and there is no lust in me for them. I don't find a plump breast enticing. No one understands how my soul cries out for hard lips and strong arms.

He turns and for a moment our eyes meet. I hope he can't see me because of the shadows I hide in, but it feels like his brilliant blue gaze burns deep into my soul and uncovers all my secret longings. My prick hardens and I blush. A small smile quirks the corner of his full lips. He knows. The most popular man in the room knows I want him. He knows I long for his lips to kiss my hand. *How can he tell?* My clothes hide the scars of my perversion. Unless it is true what my father tells me. My secret longings brand my forehead with my shame. He moves towards me.

Embarrassment and pain tear through me. The room closes in around me and I can't breathe. I need to get away. I need to run. Leaving my shelter, I stumble towards the doors leading to the garden. Maybe I could lose myself amongst the night, forget the way my body burns for him. Forget for a second what kind of freak I am. Darkness is a friend I'm very familiar with. I've often longed to become one with the dark and never worry about showing my face in the light again. Yet my father, for all that he hates and loathes me, keeps dragging me out into the world and I can't fight him.

Tears fill my eyes and blind me to the obstacles in my way. I bump into couples strolling along the edge of the dance floor. In an awkward stammer, I beg their pardon, reaching the doors at last. Sliding out into the darkness, I rush to the gazebo at the far end of the garden. It is falling apart, crumbling from neglect and indifference. It suits my mood. I suffer from neglect as well. The absence of kindness and love can cause a person's soul to wither and die.

I know what the people in the house are whispering about me. "Face of an angel and the brains of a goose." "Poor Lord Williamson. His heir is worthless." There'll be the ones who'll try to be gracious. "He's just shy. Give him a little more time. He's only been up from the country for a month or so." Yes, I've only been allowed out of my cage for a month or so. Like any creature held captive for too long, I'm unsure what to do and how to live without those bars in front of my vision.

I groan. I am worthless. People scare me and I don't want to infect them with the disease I deal with every second of my life. Burying my face in my hands, I flinch. The scars on my back cause me pain even though they aren't fresh. I still remember the feel of the whip across my shoulders as my father screamed at me about my perversion. Yet when the first beatings started, I didn't understand why he hated me so. As I grew older and encountered more men, I began to realize what perversions my father was trying to beat out of me. My skin burns. For one brief instance, I hear the whistle of the leather in the air and I cringe, feeling the cut deep in my soul.

Warm skin envelops my hands and gently tugs them away from my face. I glance up. Before I can protest or say anything, his lips meet mine and I fall.

This isn't right. The voice in my head sounds like my father. The words try to urge me to break the kiss and run away. I can't. I'm as captured by his mouth as I am by the ropes my father ties me with at night. But unlike the ropes, his touch doesn't hurt. It soothes and teases. His teeth nibble along my bottom lip and I moan.

One hand holds mine while the other buries itself in my hair. He tilts my head to the perfect angle and takes the kiss deeper. I know I should be fighting him off. I should be swearing and spitting. I should be doing all those things men do when they try to fight the passion in them, but I can't.

I might lie to the world, but I've never lied to myself. I want this. I need this. For once in my life, I'm taking what someone is willing to give. I'm not forcing this blond god to kiss me. I'm not making him touch me. He searched me out. He followed me. In a second, I'll go back to hating myself. I'll revert to the monster and freak I know in my heart I am, but just this one moment in time, I can be desired. Maybe in this brief second of space, I can be loved.

Part Two

Here I am again. Another ball on a different night. But where I had been dragged to the others, I am willing to make an appearance at this one. My uncle, the Earl, is bringing his daughter out and I must show support. Besides, my uncle is the only one of my family I feel remotely comfortable around. Maybe it's because he cares for nothing other than his horses. It might be the fact that he doesn't treat me like a leper or some untamed animal. My father hates him with almost the same passion he does me. So maybe that makes us comrades-in-arms. Or I could just be thinking this to make myself feel better.

I swing the young lady I am waltzing with around and a shot of heat runs down my spine. Lifting my gaze from the blank face of the girl, I feel lust burn through me as my eyes land on him. He enters the room as if he owns it. This time there are no shadows to hide me. He meets my stare with a nod. He recognizes me and that thought scares me. In my mind, I had hoped he wouldn't remember what my face looked like. He smiles. I stumble.

The lady protests and I mumble my abject apology. I am a complete failure at many things, but I pride myself on being a marvelous dancer. Unlike most men, my mind isn't cluttered with the scent of the woman's skin or the glistening of her lips. I can feel the music in my body and it is the only time I'm free from the world. I glance over my shoulder. He's making his way slowly around the room, greeting people, but he moves closer to where I dance.

Here is my chance to find out my mysterious lover's name. When I ask my dance partner to tell me who he is, she looks at me like I'm an idiot. I get the feeling she is wondering what rock I've been hiding under. She tells me and shock strikes me dumb. I've heard of him. Back in society after a year of mourning and on the hunt for a second wife are the rumors floating around him. My dance partner natters on about how she hopes he'll talk to her. I want to brag. I want just one person to know that I, for one moment, kissed the lips of that god. I nod and somehow in her slow mind, she realizes I don't care what she's saying.

We finish our dance in silence and I return her to her mother. My body knows what it wants. It wants to return to his arms. My lips want to be taken again by him. "No," I whisper to myself. I can't take the chance of being close to him. I manage to leave the ballroom without running into anyone or making a bigger fool of myself. No more gardens for me. I find there is no longer any comfort in the darkness of crumbling ruins. I lost my heart in a garden a week ago and haven't been able to find it again. He has tainted the beauty of the dark. Now instead of forgetting the world around me, I can only see him standing in the moonlight, staring at me with an emotion in his eyes I've never seen before.

The library offers the solace I'm seeking. I slip into the empty room and make my way to the window. Staring out, I study the couples wandering in my uncle's garden. They are bathed with silver moonlight. A pretty world I can't be a part of. It's a place of deceit and lies. A fake world graced with paper people. I've never learned to chat about anything. My education stops at the door of my father's house. The world is blank to me and I fear all the things I don't know about it.

My mind turns with determination back to him. *How did he know I would accept his touch? What told him I'd willingly give my lips to him without protest?* I rub my chest. My face reflects in the window and I search for the brand marking me. There must be something somewhere on my face telling people of the horrors I hide inside. Some symbol letting those who would hate or mock me know I am a helpless scapegoat for their cruelty. I see nothing except the blankness of my own stare. Darkness reigns in my gaze. I fear one day I'll look at myself and see nothing. One day I'll have disappeared and no one will care.

My breath fogs the window as I sigh. Somehow he sees me. On the night he kissed me, there was no cruelty in his lips and no hatred in his touch. I can still feel his skin warming my chilled body. In my dreams, I relive the moment his mouth gave me my first kiss. I feel my cheeks heat as my prick gets hard. It happens every time I think of that night and my shame grows. I press my hand against my stiff flesh. The glass fogs as I groan.

The snick of the door shutting causes me to whirl around. There he stands with his golden hair glinting in the darkness like the stars in the night sky. My voice gets stuck in my throat as he moves towards me. He shouldn't want me. He shouldn't sully his hands by touching me. I reach out a hand. *Am I telling him to stop or am I asking him to come closer?* I don't know. My mind is overloaded with thoughts and questions.

He is Lord Greyson, Duke of Northampton. He's the confidant of kings, princes, and prime ministers. He's the prize every gold-digging mother and fortune hunting father look for. To me, he is a god and as such, is out of reach as God is to a fallen angel.

He is perfection. I am a monster.

Part Three

He moves towards me and I back up. His clean hands must not touch me. The memories I have of his touch disappear behind my fear of fouling his purity. The cool window glass presses against my back and the ridges of my scars serve to remind me of our differences. His passion is wasted on a demon such as me.

"No," I whisper, holding my trembling hands out in front of me. Warning him to stay away. For all that I'm saying no, I beg him to see beyond the words to the truth hidden deep in my soul. *Do I truly corrupt everything I touch? Am I an incubus to suck the life from this vivid man?*

His Grace looks at me and I see an emotion shining in his gaze I can't name. It isn't one I have any knowledge of, but I know I desire for it to stay in his eyes. His voice slides over me like velvet. "I've seen you standing in the shadows. Aloof and unapproachable. Your eyes reflect nothing but what the world expects to see. Yet looking deeper into them, I see fear and longing. A fallen angel yearning for some glimpse of Heaven."

I shiver. *How had he managed to read my thoughts? Is it possible that he knows he is the only Heaven I ever want to embrace?* My voice sticks in my throat. God, I don't know if I'm praying for him to touch me or for him to leave. I can't protest or move as he takes my shaking hands in his.

"So cold," he murmurs, rubbing our hands together while his blue stare burns into my eyes.

My skin may be cold, but a fire is burning inside me. My heart pounds and I start to pant. I long to shut my eyes and block out his knowing gaze. I don't want him to see my shame. I try to push him away. "No. Go." My voice holds no strength. I'm such a coward; I can't say what I wish for. My father's teachings have gagged my dreams and turned them into nightmares. I want Greyson to warm me. I wish to find comfort within the circle of his strong arms.

"Go?" He laughs softly. "I find I need another taste of you, my angel."

Air brushes my lips. I breathe deep of his male scent. I harden and heat rushes through me. "Shouldn't." I sound like a fool, reduced to single word sentences, but my brain is shutting down with lust and fear. I fear he will kiss me. I fear he won't. I'm pulled in different directions, each one trying to tear me to pieces. *Why must I show my ignorance in his presence?* The duke is experienced and his lovers must be far more educated than I am. "Wrong."

"I have spent my life doing everything I should. It is time I start doing what I shouldn't, but in doing so, give myself the greatest joy." His hands creep up my arms. One goes around and cups the back of my head. The other slips to encircle my waist and tugs me close. Somehow his hand worms its way under my jacket to rest against the linen of my shirt. "There is nothing wrong with taking pleasure in each other, Angel. The only wrong would be if we denied our attraction."

I tense. His palm lies on the ridge of one of the scars crossing my back. He doesn't seem to notice the outward signs of my demon soul. Our chests brush with each breath we take. I find my gaze captured by his. Desire burns like a flame in his blue eyes. I know that emotion for I've seen it in other couples' eyes when they look at each other. This emotion isn't one I'm used to seeing directed towards me.

"Trust me," he begs as his mouth takes mine.

Trust isn't a word in my vocabulary. All of my life, those I've trusted have hurt me and turned from me. There is nothing left in my soul to allow me to trust his Grace, but the monster I harbor inside my heart wants just another taste of this man. I willingly risk God's wrath to feel Greyson's mouth on mine again. Damnation will be sweet if it comes at his touch.

As he pulls me tighter to him, I place my hands on his shoulders. Blood pounds. Lust burns. My pulse roars in my ears. His mouth is firm, but he treats me like crystal. Maybe he senses I'll shatter at the slightest wrong move. His tongue bathes my bottom lip. He uses my gasp as permission to stroke our tongues together. He teases the roof of my mouth, creating shivers of lust to rush down my spine. Pleasure swims through me. Nothing has prepared me for the need building in me simply from his kiss. My prick swells until it threatens to burst from my breeches. Never have I been this hard and I ache with want.

My head reels from the taste of him. Angry voices whisper in my mind. I shake, tension seeping into my muscles. He brings our hips together and our pricks rub against each other. For the first time, I feel the evidence of another man's desire for me. He rocks against me and I moan. His heat is melting me. I want to sink deep into him and allow him to swallow me until I become a part of him. His fingers caress my back. The pressure of his palm on my scar reminds me of my insanity. The whistle of leather through the air and the crack of the whip against tender skin tears my mind apart. Wrenching away from him, I clench my teeth to keep from crying out.

"Hell." He pulls back.

A drop of blood wells from his lip. Before his finger can touch it, I run. My glimpse of Heaven reminds me that my place is in Hell.

Part Four

It has been two days since the disastrous kiss in my uncle's library. Somehow I've managed to avoid going to any balls. I can't help but wonder if Greyson looks for me at the parties. Does he long to touch me again?

I slip from the house in the first hours of morning. I'll miss breakfast with my father, but it won't matter. My family doesn't miss my presence. I'm not part of their world except to belittle and abuse. The early morning fog carpets the ground in front of me as I ride my gelding in Hyde Park. Besides dancing, I seem to have a talent for horses. While at the ancestral home, I spend what free time I have riding. It's the only way I get any freedom from my prison walls. My horse is well-mannered so my mind twists and turns my encounters with the duke.

The memories of our kiss drive me crazy with lust. Late at night I ache to be held in his arms again. Then I'd feel the tortured skin on my back and realize my infection has somehow poisoned his Grace.

It's the only explanation I have for his searching me out and touching me. I've bewitched him. My father's words are true. I am the devil's spawn. I've corrupted a god and perverted him. A heaving sob rises in my chest. Once more I wonder why I didn't die when my father begged me to after the wounds from my whipping festered. Why hang on to a life without joy or love? Why did God allow my uncle to save me when I tried to end it all? Was this some form of punishment from the Father for my secrets?

I'm buried deep in my thoughts and don't hear him approach until his gloved hand appears before my eyes to touch my own hand.

"Angel." His voice is warm.

My gaze shoots to his face and horror fills my heart at the wound on his lip. Without thought, my fingers caress the air over it. He doesn't flinch.

"I'm sorry." Tears slip down my cheek. Ducking my head, I grimace. It's bad enough he's guessed my secret longings. He must think I'm weak with all the tears I shed around him. Why does he make the emotions come to the surface? I endure terrible things at the hands of my father without breaking down, yet I can't be around Greyson for a minute without sobbing.

"Don't be sorry. It's a small price to pay to be able to taste you." He grabs my hand and lays our entwined fingers on his thigh.

Glancing wildly around, I try to free myself. "Your Grace, we mustn't be seen like this." Fear tracks down my spine, branching off into each scar until every muscle tenses. Even though I'm terrified of someone seeing us, I find myself tracing his thigh and the seam of his riding breeches.

"We are the only ones out here. I like touching you."

I feel my face heat as he takes off his glove. After he strips mine from my hand, we touch skin-to-skin for the first time. His skin is rough as if he has done work without protecting them. His flesh is warm and slowly I begin to thaw again. Greyson seems to be the only one whose touch doesn't leave me cold. I'm paralyzed as I watch him lift my fingers to his mouth. The angry voice living in my head yells at me to pull my hand away. It demands I tell a lie and say I don't want his Grace to touch me.

My soul ignores it. The part of me I've hidden deep to avoid punishment wants to enjoy its time in the sun. His tongue swirls around my fingertips as if he's tasting his favorite dessert. Tremors wrack my body and my horse shifts beneath me, reacting to the tightening of my muscles. I feel lust flood my skin as I begin to understand the depth of my depravity. I want his mouth to take my prick instead of my fingers. I need his tongue to taste my seed instead of my sweat even though I've never been serviced like that before.

Greyson's blue eyes darken and I know he's reacting to the desire that must be burning in mine. I break my gaze from his face and glance lower. The large bulge between his thighs makes my shaft twitch and swell. I long to touch him.

"We shouldn't," I whisper, barely loud enough to hear over my pounding heart.

Releasing my fingers from his mouth, he asks, "Why not?"

"It's wrong." There's certainty in my voice. This conviction has been beaten into me over the course of several years.

"Who says it is?"

His strong grip takes my hand and places it where I long for it to be the most. Without thought, I stroke him through his breeches. He groans. I measure his length with my fingers, touching gently even though I wish permission to feel it unclothed in my hand.

"Society. The priests. They all whisper and call this perversion."

I fear what society and the church can do to me, but the fear doesn't stop me as I press my palm harder against him.

He shifts slightly and moves in counter-point to my strokes. My inexperience makes my hand pause. Is this what he wants? Or is he trying to make me stop? His words come out in a harsh whisper.

"I married a woman I didn't love and shared her bed until she gave me two sons, whom I love, but rarely see. Then I turned from her, leaving her with a broken heart. I've done what society and the church says I should." He stops and grabs my hand. Silence reigns until I meet his eyes.

"All doing my duty has brought me is pain and shame. I no longer care if I lose any of what they say is important. Honor to myself now means more. I can lose it all and not miss what my life was."

His blue eyes beg me to understand what he's saying, but I'm not sure I can. What does he want from me? Why has he chosen me? Doubt floods my mind. Is it really me that he wants? Does he search for the worse outcast that will get him exiled from the ton?

Hoof-beats float down the trail towards us. Greyson kisses

my hand and lets me go. Before he disappears into the morning mist, he gives me a sad smile and asks, "What have you got to lose?"

Part Five

"What have you got to lose?"

His question burns in my mind. I sit at the table and listen to my father rant about me going to the ball tonight. For the first time, I want to scream at him to shut the hell up. It is an odd urge for me since I never risk his wrath by speaking back. I'm dressed and sitting at the table instead of hiding. For one moment in my life, I am doing just exactly as he wishes and yet he isn't happy. I can't help but wonder if there is a reason why he wants me to go, or are the rumors flying about the absence of his heir?

I'm going to the ball because it's the only way I know to contact his Grace. My courage doesn't extend to visiting his house. I'm not sure my courage will last long enough for me to tell him I have nothing to lose. Not one damn thing that anyone can take from me. Not even my life is my own. Father owns that entirely, yet he doesn't see the mutiny taking place deep inside me. I want to find Greyson and tell him when you're empty you have nothing to lose.

It's difficult to admit that fact to myself. It's heart wrenching and painful. Much like amputating a limb would be, I imagine. My family surrounds me, but I'm not a part of them. They are living their lives in the narrow confines of the society they love. I'm not living at all. I'm merely existing, pushed outside of their circle and watching them as if they were actors on stage, playing at being loving, caring people. There are times when I want to whisper to the nearest person about the lie they are living. Society sees my father as wanting only the best for me, but only I know the truth of the whips, chains, and ropes. Only I am given a chance to see the hate living deep in their souls. A hate for everyone, not just me, though I bear the brunt of it most of the time.

Staring at my father, I feel a strange weight lift from my chest. All my life I feared losing his love and respect. Then I catch a glimpse of the marks on my back and I realize I never had them.

I remember the rope burns on my ankles and feel the pain just his voice can inflict. He hates me and always has. Nothing I do will ever bring that back to me. Not once has a kind hand been held out to me. Not even my mother cares what happens to me. She turned her back on me the day I was born and has never looked at me since. I've begged her for help and she walks from me as if she's deaf or blind to my agony. My younger siblings aren't allowed to have any contact with me, as if I will infect them with whatever disease I carry.

A stinging slap captures my attention. Quickly I drop my gaze. My father sees any confidence in me as a direct challenge. I had been staring at him while lost in thought. As a matter of habit, I run my finger over the angry marks on my wrist. They are symbols of my last desperate cry for acknowledgement. If not for my uncle, I would have bled to death and that is another reason why I feel some obligation to him. Whether he knows of my affliction or not, he still welcomes me with some sort of warmth. For a moment, I think about the stricken look in my uncle's face when he found me curled on the floor of the study, a dark pool of blood under my wrists. My uncle called for the doctor. He was the only one who seemed worry about me. My father would have mourned in public, but rejoiced in private at my death.

I tune Father out as he begins his tirade. In my mind, I imagine Greyson's face. I recreate the touch of his lips and the feel of his body against mine. In the night, he keeps me company and my body yearns to feel him closer to me. I want to share more than kisses with him. Before meeting him, my dreams were demon-infested nightmares, driving me mad inch by terrifying inch. Now in the weeks since meeting him, those images have changed to dreams of the two of us somewhere safe. Some place my father has no access to and therefore can't harm the duke. In this place, Greyson takes me in his arms and kisses me. He loves me and makes my body ache for a release I have no name for.

I flush and my father glares at me. It's as if he knows what my thoughts are. One of the footmen sets a plate in front of me and I brush his sleeve on accident. He flinches away. If a mere servant can't bear being near me, how can such a man like the duke suffer my touch?

Yet he revels in it and seems willing to do whatever he must to feel my hands again. My soul hungers for his taste and heat. If I'm depraved and insane, I will wallow in my perversions with a glad heart as long as he is with me. His touch is kind and gentle. Though I have spent precious little time with him, he sees me for what I really am and he doesn't turn from me. I long for him to embrace my lonely soul and show me that I'm not a freak. I want him to prove my father's words wrong. I'm not the devil's spawn. I won't destroy everything I love. I can survive outside the cage they have forced me to live in.

Lord Greyson has given me the keys to my freedom with two kisses and a sad smile.

Part Six

This night I scour the swirling crowd. I search with anxious eyes for the man I'm becoming infatuated with. I try not to think about what will happen if Greyson doesn't show. *Will my courage and anger hold long enough for me to wait until tomorrow night?* I don't think so. I have the uneasy feeling tonight is my only night to reach out and take what I want. The duke is a shooting star that streaked across my night sky for a brief moment and if I look away, he'll have gone on to some other universe.

"Got your eye on anyone, son?"

I stiffen and turn to see my uncle standing beside me. His bluff face and jovial manner make my father despise him, but there has always been something safe about him for me. It has nothing to do with his saving my life. It's because he tries to see me. Unlike the other members of my family, he doesn't look through me as if I am a piece of glass.

"No, sir." God, I hope I'm not that obvious. Please don't let my father see me looking for someone. I don't want him to come over to me and ask about the girl I might be interested in. He would know if I lie and my punishment will be worse if I don't.

"Just as well. The cream of the crop is your cousin and we can't have you two getting married." He laughs and slaps my shoulder in jest. He's right though, I've only observed this year's marriageable girls with no thought to finding one of my own. I admit my young cousin is beautiful. Many people comment that we look enough alike to be twins. I laugh when I hear those words. She's beautiful and innocent. I'm hideous and depraved. There can be no comparison between us.

I manage a slight smile, trying not to wince. My father had shoved me into the wall earlier in the day, leaving a bruise at the spot my uncle hit. One of many I've managed to cover up with clothes and lies.

"A rather unattractive crop of fillies this season," he continues, either not noticing or not caring about my discomfort. A smile chases its way over my face. My uncle equating the noble ladies to horses makes my heart happy for a second.

A wave of heat surrounds me as if my clothes have caught on fire. He is here. Moving through the room, he greets lord and lady alike, showing no favor to any. My heart begins to pound. Sweat beads on my forehead. The moment of my freedom moves closer with each step he takes towards me. *Will my fear take this chance from me?* A gasp of excitement escapes my lips.

I take a step toward him, his laughter calling to me like a siren does to the sailors on the sea. I meet resistance. Looking down, I see my uncle's hand on my arm. His hand grasps me tight and stays my rush to the duke. I want to shake his grip off me. My soul is getting tired of being restrained. I look up to see Uncle studying me with deep interest.

Panic, fear, and shame shoot through me. Does he know? Has my father voiced his displeasure in me to my uncle? I'm not sure why or how Father would do that since he hasn't spoken to Uncle except for polite words said in public.

"Careful, son." Uncle's gaze swings from me to where the duke stands. There is nothing in his eyes to warn me how he feels. "You must learn to play their games."

"I don't know what you're talking about," I force through my panic.

"You know what I'm saying. Come see me tomorrow. We've much to discuss." He squeezes my arm and turns to leave. Looking back over his shoulder, he says, "I live in a glass house as well, son. There'll be no stones thrown by me."

I struggle to grasp what he says to me. There is a memory fighting to free itself in my mind, but all I can think of is Greyson strolling towards me. My heart pounds and my blood boils. My throat closes and I find I'm fighting to pull air into my lungs. A shiver of fear rolls through me. What if he doesn't want me anymore? What if he's changed his mind?

"Breathe," I whisper to myself.

Uncle's warning wings through my deprived brain. Fainting at his Grace's feet isn't being careful. It would bring attention to both of us. I don't think I could survive the stares and laughter. Though it isn't my own reputation I worry about. I don't want to make the duke a laughing stock. I don't want him ridiculed for my silly infatuation.

"You're here." His tone is soft so no one can hear him.

"Yes," I want to scream. "I'm here, breaking free of the life they want me to live."

"What have you got to lose?" He repeats his question.

Silence reigns between us. I'm choking on my answer. I know it'll change my life, no matter what I say. There is no one else in the room with us, even though we are surrounded by the ton. No sound is heard though an orchestra plays in the background.

Greyson is standing before me, holding the keys to the lock for my heart. He's reaching out to risk the devil and open my cage door. My hand wants to touch him. My lungs want to breathe his air. My mouth wants to taste his lips again.

I want to speak. My soul begs my mouth to open; begs my throat to allow the words out. Fear has clamped its claws deep into my flesh and shame stands guard to keep me from busting free.

Emotions flash in his blue eyes and I'm not sure if they are anger, hurt, or sadness. So many emotions I know the intimate touch of, but have never seen in anyone's eyes.

He nods and moves away, disappointment on his face. That's one expression I recognize, having seen it on my father's face all my life. I want to stop him. I want to hold out my hand and touch him. The weight of the stares holds me back. In God's entire world, there is no creature more pathetic than me.

Part Seven

Greyson disappears into the crowd. My heart breaks. A god within my grasp and like a fool I let him go. A scream builds in my chest. I want to cry out to him. I fight to stay on my feet. Falling to my knees and begging him to come back would only bring about the end of my captivity, but not in any pleasant way. I steel my backbone and lock my legs, trying to look indifferent to the whole episode.

Frozen to the spot, I ignore people moving around me except to cringe when they get too close. I'm caught in a whirlpool of anger. It swirls and flares. My anger focuses on Greyson first for not understanding my silence. Then it whips around to berate me next for having no sense of worth.

For it is doubt keeping me from tracking him down. How can a man so full of life and confidence want a shell like me? All that I might ever be has been ripped from me. He calls me Angel. I call myself monster. Once long ago, I didn't think of myself as a monster. The word freak meant nothing to me. Now those words are the description of my true self and they hurt more than anyone will know. A man like Greyson shouldn't even step in the same room with me.

A hand clamps down on my bruised shoulder and I bite my tongue to keep from crying out. I know who it is from the cruelty in his touch. This hand deals out anger and pain with a flick of a wrist. Flinching, I know tonight's punishment will be severe. Before Father can say anything, my pretty cousin is beside us.

"This is our dance." She beams up at my father. Her face is happy and confident. Her father indulges her in everything and she's sure there is no evil in her world. I allow her that illusion. I wouldn't hurt her or destroy her dreams for anything.

While my father hates my uncle, he can't deny my uncle's daughter, so he allows her to drag me away. We melt into the dancing couples until we've moved beyond his sight. She tugs me into an alcove. I long to leave. My mind wonders how I can sneak away without my father finding out. I'd have a few minutes of peace before he comes home.

"What is the matter with you?" She glares up at me. "Poppa sent me to save you. He could see your father growing furious with you. How could you snub his Grace like that?" Her dark brown curls bob while she shakes her head at me.

It always comes down to me being the bad one. I'm the incompetent fool who is single-handedly destroying the family name. She's so young and innocent. I don't want to taint her with my foulness. I shrug and move away. I don't want to talk to her, but she has never been cruel to me either. Tonight might be the first time we've spent more than a second together since she was born. I'm amazed at how grown-up she is. Any man will be lucky to get her. She'll have love and I'll have nothing because of my fear. I'm making myself sick. I want to drown my sorrow in brandy.

While we dance, a commotion starts at the entrance to the ballroom. We glance over, and my cousin gasps.

"Marissa must be beside herself. They actually got the Gypsy Devil to show up."

"Gypsy Devil? Who is he and why do they call him that?" I concentrate on asking my questions. At least she's no longer talking about Greyson.

"It's all quite scandalous really," she whispers. "He's the bastard son of an Earl, but his father has always recognized him as his issue. Even brought the boy to raise at his country house. When he was sixteen, he ran away. Just returned to London after ten years, richer than Crocus, yet no one knows how he made his money."

"But his name can't be Devil or anything like that," I protest, turning my gaze to study the dark-haired, dark-eyed man standing among a crowd of eager supplicants. Yet something in the way he held his shoulders tells me he would rather be anywhere else besides the ballroom.

She snorts. "Of course not. It's Lord Bertram Wilkins. Everyone calls him the Gypsy Devil because his mother was a Gypsy girl who seduced the Earl."

A movement from the edge of the crowd surrounding Lord Wilkins catches my gaze, and I watch Greyson approach the lord. They greet each other like they are good friends, and a surge of jealousy rushes through me. Foolish really, considering I'd ruined my chance at having anything more than a few stolen kisses from the duke.

"Lord Greyson is the most handsome man in the room." Her brown eyes, so much like mine, twinkle with a sly light. "Quite rich and friends with all sorts of important people. His wife would hold a high place in society. I'd take a shot at him. Too bad his interest is already captured."

"Captured? By whom? How do you know? Who is it?" I blurt out. My tone is frantic and jealous. She chuckles and I realize she's figured something out. The minx has tricked me. I search out a way to leave her.

Giving me a cunning little smile, she backs me into the shadows. "I've heard rumors about the duke."

"Rumors?" I find I don't want to hear what she has to say.

"Wicked rumors. Some say the handsome duke has no use for the fairer sex. He likes his lovers to be harder and more like him." She shoots me a look with a raised eyebrow as if asking me to confirm what she's been hearing.

My breath comes in bursts and spots swim before my eyes. I didn't give our secret away, my mind screams. Oh God, they all know. Somehow the depravity brewing inside me has been seen and it's destroying the duke's reputation. Maybe it is better that I didn't say anything to him about having nothing to lose.

My cousin gives me a wink. "Who would've thought my competition would be my own cousin?" She touches my wrist where my self-inflicted scar is. Her touch sears my skin.

I can almost feel my skin split again. I remember the overwhelming pain and helplessness I felt when I watched my blood pool under my hands. By the time my uncle found me, I had grown cold and happy. The breaking of my chains was only one more drop away. He saved me, but tonight I've destroyed any chance I might have with the duke. My perversion has touched him and tainted his soul. Others are whispering and talking about him. It's my fault. It's all my fault.

Bile rises from my stomach. Her eyes widen and she points to a potted plant we are hiding behind. Throwing myself to my knees, I heave. There is nothing for me to purge for I haven't eaten in a day or two. Yet it feels as if I'm emptying everything from my body. Every emotion I might have had is leaving my body. My brain is screaming my perfidy. Chance lost. Life denied.

Heart, soul, brain, and nerves go. Blackness starts to descend and I wonder if I've given up. There's no point in living when my god has turned his back on me.

Part Eight

Sensation returns in waves. Voices are whispering. I'm floating, held together by two strong arms. Harsh words. Father. I cringe.

No, I shout from my silence. *Don't let him touch me.* His touch will hurt. His hands cause me pain and make me bleed. I don't want that anymore. I need to get away somehow. The duke has shown me another world where words don't hurt and people care. I want to be part of that world, yet it might only be in my fantasies.

One voice separates from the noise. It rumbles under my ear. I try to get closer, for something in my memory tells me this voice will not hurt. Even in my confusion, I know the owner of this voice cares for me. I've never heard words spoken in anger from him.

Words become more distinct. I hear Father argue with Uncle. I wonder why their voices hold such urgency. Why would they even be talking to each other? Father can barely stand to be in the same room with my uncle.

I begin to wonder if I have died. It would explain why Father and Uncle are talking. The warm safe feeling I have could be because I'm held in the arms of an angel who's carrying me to Heaven. I laugh to myself. I'll not be getting to Heaven. Hell is the only place for me.

Cold washes over my face and I force my eyes open. Concern fills the brilliant blue eyes looking down at me. He hasn't abandoned me. For some reason, he chooses to stay close to me.

My cousin's brown eyes invade my view. "Poppa, he's awake." She glances over her shoulder at someone else.

I look around. No longer am I hiding behind a potted plant. I'm outside. I realize I'm in Greyson's arms, leaning against him. Horror fills me and I try to push away from him, but he won't let me. The duke's arms tighten around me and he shakes his head.

Father and Uncle stand staring at me. Father's eyes are filled with scorn and disgust. There is so much hate in his heart for me. I wonder if it's not as black as his soul. Uncle's eyes are worried.

"All you ever do is embarrass me. Why am I cursed with a son like you?" Father reaches for my arm. His hand resembles a claw that will tear out what's left of my heart. If I go back, I know I will never live out the year.

I shrink from his fearsome touch. Turning, I bury my face in Greyson's chest. No more. It no longer matters to me what people think. There's no will left in me to fight. My father has achieved his goal. He has crushed me. Who knew the destruction would come not with fists but with words? Who knew the final blow would be delivered from the smiling lips of my cousin? She doesn't even know she's destroyed me.

Greyson hands me to my uncle. A spike of surprise finds its birth in me when Uncle waves to his carriage driver. I glance up at him. His serious face tells me he means what he is saying.

"You'll come home with me."

There is no argument from me. I never want to see Father's house again. So much pain and agony reside there. I turn my gaze back to Greyson and Father.

"I suggest you go back inside, Williamson. We mustn't create a bigger scene than this has already become." Greyson's voice is harsh and commanding.

I've never heard anyone talk to Father like that.

"I've heard about you. There's no way I'll allow you to corrupt my son. He'll not be your catamite." Father speaks in a soft tone, trying to insure no one hears him.

"And everything spoken by the forked tongues of the ton is true. You don't want him to come with me so you can keep him as your whipping boy." Sarcasm drips from his Grace's words.

Father flushes. "It matters not. He's still my son."

"He's reached his majority, Brother. If he no longer wishes to dwell under your roof, you can't force him." Uncle reminds

Father.

Uncle is right. I'm twenty-three now and if I could have broken free earlier, I would have left my family's house, even if it meant walking the streets. Each time I thought about it, Father would tie me down and add another link to the heavy chain he bound me with.

I tune out the words. My eyes focus on Greyson's face. Is it just my hopeful wish that there seems to be caring in his eyes when he looks at me? Is it possible my silence didn't destroy his regard for me? I shiver.

"My carriage is here. I'll be taking my nephew to my house." Uncle glances at my cousin. "You started this mess. Go and tell them your cousin is sick. Lady Acksinbury will escort you home."

My cousin whispers "I'm sorry" in my ear. She is able to get Father to take her back inside. I know I've not seen the last of my father. He doesn't want to add more rumors than are already flying tonight. But he won't let me go so easily.

Greyson helps Uncle get me in the carriage. My legs don't seem to want to work. Curling up on the seat, I hide in the corner. The shadows welcome me and I find I can breathe once more. The air seems cleaner than before. Is it because there is less oppression?

The duke's blue eyes reassure me as he speaks to my uncle. "I'll follow you home."

Uncle makes no objection. I find myself wondering why Father despises my uncle. His disdain must have roots back beyond my birth. I have no memory of them ever acting like brothers. Though I do remember summers I spent at my uncle's house while Father and Mother visited friends.

The door clicks shut. Instead of feeling like I am trapped again, freedom seems just a carriage ride away. Is it possible the bars holding me away from the world can be broken so quickly? How will I handle the world without hatred?

Part Nine

Exhaustion sets in. My head aches. I wish for peace, just a moment of silence that I've never had before. Shutting my eyes, I try to ignore my uncle sitting across from me in the carriage.

"I won't bother you tonight, son, but we must talk. Greyson seems to have staked a claim and you need to make a decision." There's a knowing look in Uncle's eyes.

A decision? There's nothing to decide really. He seems to think I have options. I can't help but laugh. Where will I go if Uncle doesn't take me in? As for the duke staking a claim, I don't believe that. I think he's just being nice to a pathetic creature. I've burned bridges with my father. He'll disown me for sure now that Uncle has come to my aid. Besides, even if fear holds me back from ever confessing my love to the Duke, I have made my decision not to hide the truth, at least not from myself.

"No choice. I'll go to debtor's prison before I set another foot in that house." For the first time, courage has taken hold and forces me to cut the chains holding me down. I'm sure it is false courage and won't last beyond the time it takes for us to get to my Uncle's home.

"Brave words. You've never lived without money or a roof over your head. Do you have the strength to reach out for what you want the most? Or has my brother beaten the heart out of you?" Uncle seems concerned, yet my mind asks me where he was all those years while I was abused for reasons I didn't understand.

I shrug and turn to look out the carriage window. I don't fear being without money or shelter. I don't even fear not having food to eat. There have been times when I've gone days without eating. I fear returning to the prison I'm running from.

The rattle of a wheel over the stone draws my attention. I'm aware of the other vehicle traveling behind. Another carriage carrying my salvation or my doom. There's no way of knowing which one he'll be. If he is my doom, then I'll accept it with open arms because I've never felt safer than when I'm in his arms. I'm not sure if there is salvation for one such as I.

"Why?" The question explodes from my mouth. "Why are you helping me? You've never cared before."

A sigh escapes my uncle's lips. The faint light from the lantern on the outside of the carriage shows a suspicious shine in his eyes. He can't be crying for me. No one has shed tears over me in years.

"History shouldn't be allowed to repeat itself. Helping you might erase some black marks against me. For the first time I can see past my own sorrow. The duke has opened my eyes to the pain my brother is causing."

A memory glimmers in my mind, but I can't grasp it. I don't understand and my head aches too much for me to pursue his words. My heart aches as well. I feel as if I'm wallowing in the ocean with no anchor. The darkness swirls and ebbs around me. Strange sounds fill my mind. The need to run rises in me. The voices mock me. They swear and abuse me. Mixed in with their insults are the burn of the lash and the cut of the knife. My back burns. No thought in my mind except to escape them.

I'm surrounded by a torrent of blackness, taking me from the flimsy safety of the carriage. My mind surrenders to the emotions and all I can think of is that I must get away. My uncle is taking me back to my father. He's lied to me, like everyone in my life does. He doesn't want me. He wishes only to hurt me. Soon it will be his hand wielding the whip. It will be his laughter that abuses my ears. I must get away.

The carriage stops. Without thinking, I throw open the door and jump. I run past Greyson's carriage, ignoring the shouts of my uncle.

"Come back here. You'll hurt yourself."

I run into the brick wall at the opening of the alley. I don't feel the pain of my knuckles scraping against the stone. Any protests my uncle and Greyson might have are drowned by the noise in my head. The sounds resolve themselves into words said in my father's voice. Names he has called me since I was ten.

"Pervert."

"Freak."

"Monster."

Each word cracks against my back. It flays my mind and all I can do is run. Running from pain. Fleeing from hate. There is no way anyone could care for me. My father's voice tells me the duke has lied to me. He doesn't care about me. Greyson plans on using me until I'm empty, then he'll abandon me to the void.

Demons nip at my heels, driving me farther from the light, deeper into the darkness. I glance over my shoulder to see who is chasing me. In the shadows, I see glints of red eyes watching me. On the still night air, I hear the clicking of claws on the stone. The demons have come to drag me back with them.

§ § § §

Under the moonlight, Greyson stands watching me run away. He holds out a hand. There is a supplication in his gesture as if he is pleading for me to come back. Even though I'm too far away, I swear I hear him call out to me.

"Angel."

His voice follows me as I slip into another alleyway and it's too late. I'm lost amongst the hopeless. Maybe in the shadows of the streets, I'll find some peace from the monsters haunting my every step. If I find a place to hide, they might go back to Hell and leave me be. In my heart, I don't believe that is true. I know they will find me and tear me to pieces. I'm trying to escape from my father. I'm running from my terror, but also fleeing from Greyson's love.

Part Ten

The shadows hold demons. Things I've always known existed, yet have never seen. Hands grasp me, trying to pull me deep into their hell. I cry, trying to find a way out of the maze I've been driven into.

Footsteps sound behind me. My mind sobs in fear. They are coming for me. Chains and whips are being prepared. I'll be destroyed. Tripping, I sprawl. My clumsiness gives them a chance to catch me. Clawed hands reach for me.

"No," I sob. No more. I want to beg. I want to bargain so I don't have to return to that dungeon.

Their words are garbled. My mind, pushed beyond endurance, hides what they're saying to me. My arms are grabbed. I scream as their touch burns my skin. It feels as if brands have been pushed against my flesh. My mind conjures up the scent of sulfur.

I jerk away, scurrying to hide in the corner. I must still be in an alley for walls are closing in. Tucking my head under my arms, I turn my back to the demons. More scars will appear after they are finished. It matters little now what they do to me.

"I'm sorry."

The words drift on the dank night air. For a moment, I believe I utter them. I've spent all of my life apologizing for the very air I breathe. One of the shadows kneels beside me and I cower further into the corner. I fear returning to my father more than I fear the touch of any demon. My father has perfected the ways to try and break me. To make me beg for his mercy so he can deny me. This is no demon that kneels beside me. This is a man who will take me back to my pain.

"So sorry."

Guilt fills those words, but they don't come from me. With a caution born of numerous encounters, I raise my head enough to look the monster in the face. Clear features are bathed in a strange gold light as if something wishes me to recognize the angel that has come for me.

A sad blue gaze stares back at me. He kneels in the filth and refuse littering the ground. He ignores the menacing shades gathering around us. He reaches out a trembling hand. I don't back away this time. There is a small part of my mind that is still aware of reality. It's telling me I know this man. I know his touch and yearn for it again. He will not hurt me. Yet I'm unsure. Demons can take on the guise of man.

"I've been selfish." His smile is filled with anger, but it isn't directed at me. "I pushed and led you where I wanted you to go. I never thought about you or your feelings. I didn't think how frightening stepping from your cage could be. I broke free of mine a long time ago."

His naked palm cups my face. I close my eyes, nuzzling into his hand. He scares me. The path he wishes me to travel frightens me. Yet for all my fear, I know he won't hurt me. Not like my father does. My hurt will come when he realizes the true depth of my insanity and turns from me. Our time together will be brief before chains become the only thing holding me. Father will come for me.

"Why?" I can't help but ask. It is the same question I ask my uncle. Who am I to them that I deserve their care?

"Why you?" His other hand encircles my waist and helps me stand.

I sense the presence of my uncle. Glancing around, I see him, waiting at the alley entrance. Though I can't see his face, I detect something in the way he holds his body. It seems as if Uncle is concerned about me.

"Yes." Actual sentences are beyond my tongue. My brain is trying to figure out what is really happening. I need to find out where reality and my delusion meet.

"I wish to tell you. To open my heart to you and let you see everything, but I would have you taken care of and tucked in bed. My pushing has taken a toll on you." Greyson supports my body as we move towards the carriages.

Uncle makes no protest when Greyson helps me into his own carriage. I touch my uncle's sleeve, letting him know I'm all right for that moment in time. My knees buckle and I sit, too tired to worry about being close to the duke. I wish to hide away from the world. I want the comfort of a room and the warmth of a bed. I just want to be normal again.

"He'll come home with me." Greyson's voice holds a subtle command.

I see my uncle nod. "It's best. I can't deny my brother entrance to my house, so he'll be safe from his father with you."

I feel my uncle's gaze rest on me for a second but it's too much effort to meet his eyes.

"Be gentle with him, Greyson. For all that he is an adult, his life has been lived in a prison of his father's making. You'll have to help him understand who he really is. You'll have to undo years of abuse and brainwashing." Uncle reaches through the open door and squeezes my hand. "I'll see you tomorrow."

I acknowledge his words. Maybe he can explain the hatred my father holds for us both. Greyson shakes Uncle's hand and climbs in to sit beside me. His arm wraps around my shoulders and I settle as close to him as I can. His chin rests on my head. I feel his sigh ruffle my hair.

"Let's go home, Angel. I'll restore you to Heaven even if it means letting you go." Sadness coats his words. A trembling hand strokes my arm.

I don't believe those words. Deep inside my agony grows. I'm terrified. I have become too accustomed to Hell to ever feel comfortable in Heaven.

Part Eleven

I think I fell asleep on the ride to Greyson's home. The last thing I remember is the warmth of his body and the soothing touch of his hands. For what feels like the first time in my life, I don't worry about anyone finding me and taking advantage of my vulnerability. In his arms, I'm as safe as I can ever be.

Sounds penetrate my sleep. I fight to keep from opening my eyes. I don't want to return to the nightmare of my reality. I'm afraid last night is part of a fevered dream. As much as I fight, the voices are pulling me back into the waking world.

"I think we should have the doctor come and check him." My uncle's voice makes its way into my mind.

"There's nothing wrong with him that relaxation and being away from Williamson won't fix." The duke sounds firm, as if he really does understand my problems. How is it possible? He doesn't really know me. We've never talked. Not like normal people would.

I betray my conscious state by stretching my legs. Two shadows fall over me as I open my eyes. I shrink away before I remember who they are. Too many times I'd opened my eyes to find my father staring at me with fear and anger in his eyes.

Greyson settles on the bed, his knee pressed to my side. Relief shines in his eyes. "You're safe."

His words comfort me even though I didn't know I needed to hear them. Safe? How could I be when I knew my father would find a way into the duke's house to take me away? I'd never be safe as long as I lived.

"How long?" Once again I'm reduced to simple words around him. His confidence and strength intimidate me. I've never met a man like him. He must think me slow, but I can't bring myself to care.

"Most of the day. I think last night strained your nerves." His fingers caress my cheek.

"My life." Nothing else makes its way past the lump in my throat. I'm not sure what I mean. I turn my head to press my cheek against his palm. The rough skin there causes my skin to tingle. I find myself wishing for a kiss.

Greyson nods. "You're right. Your life has been a bit of a strain, but no more. You're safe and away from that bastard. He can't hurt you anymore." His hand holds my face in a gentle grip as if he's holding a priceless vase.

The conviction in his voice touches me. Yet I know the truth. Staring over the duke's shoulder, I see that my uncle knows as well. My father will do anything to recapture me and cage me again. It matters little to him that Greyson is a duke. My father will destroy this man while risking the wrath of kings.

"Won't give up." My heart races. I don't want to bring sorrow or pain to this man.

I could no more hurt him than I could deliberately rip wings off butterflies. My blue-eyed god is the only person ever to look at me and see my soul. He is the only human on Earth that hasn't turned from me in disgust. I would end my life before I ruined his.

"Good for you. Giving up would only allow your father to win." Greyson reaches for a glass resting on the nightstand.

Slipping his arm around my shoulders, he helps me sit up. I'm engulfed by his scent. An intriguing mixture of sweat, whisky, and earth. I bury my face against his neck and breath deep. Am I trying to memorize the smell? Will remembering it sustain me when I return to my prison? If I were taken away from him at this moment, I would remember every word he's said and every time he's touched me. His memory would bring light into the darkness.

"Drink this." He pulls back and places the glass to my lips.

I shake my head. I've been drugged too many times to trust a simple glass of water. An innocent gesture of caring would be turned into a play for power. More often than not my father would drug me to keep me from running away. My instinct is to not trust any gesture of warmth.

"Trust me, Angel. It is only water. I'll never lie to you." His lips brush my ear.

This time I don't search my uncle's face. I study the duke's. The expression I see is one I believe no one else has been granted. It's true. So far he has never lied to me and I don't think he would start now. I drink the water.

He helps me lie back down, but doesn't move away. I roll on my side and curl around his back. He's warm and I'm shivering from the chill of worry and exhaustion. Uncle clears his throat.

"What he means, your grace, is my brother won't give up. He'll do whatever he must to reclaim the boy."

Greyson frowns. "Why?"

Uncle shrugs. He seems to be unsure how to explain how my father thinks.

"I'm his." Those two words tell the truth of my father's feelings towards me. He hates and loathes me. He would gladly kill me if he could. I embarrass him, but I carry his name and for that reason alone, I am his.

"My brother is a possessive man. He will never allow his son to exist outside his control."

"Madness." The duke trembles, but whether from anger or fear, I don't know.

"Yes it is, but he has always been this way. So you must be careful, Greyson, if you mean to shelter the lad. His father can be a formidable foe."

I close my eyes. The conversation doesn't interest me. Maybe it's because deep inside I don't believe I'll ever be free of my father. I carry the scars of his hatred with me on my back. They link me to him in the most primal way possible: life and death.

It is his seed that gave me life and it will be his hand that brings me death. I have always believed this. When Father is done playing with me, he'll kill me. I accept this as my fate. I reach out and touch the duke's thigh. Until the end comes, my soul demands that I live for myself, and with the door to my cage open, I'll find freedom and love for a little while.

Darkness begins to fill my mind. I'm tired of talking. I'm tired of worrying. Tired of yearning for love and running from it as well. My last thought as I drift to sleep is maybe I'm just tired of living.

Part Twelve

Something soft brushes my lips and I moan. The touches call me from the darkness along with the voice whispering in my ear. For a second I fight. Darkness is safe. No whips or chains hold me there. No angry words cut like knives into my soul.

"Angel" whispers against my cheek. A voice calls like a siren, luring me from my safe ship to chance wrecking in the sea. Like the sailors in the myths, I fight to keep from following that voice, but something in it calls to my soul and I float to the surface of my mind.

Forcing my eyes open, I see Greyson lying next to me. He smiles and my heart skips. Without thinking of the consequences, I trace his lips with a trembling finger. He sucks the tip in and bathes it with his tongue. A low moan tears from me as sensations rocket through me. My prick gets hard and I flush, remembering how I wanted him to take my cock in his mouth while we were in the park.

"You're beautiful when you blush, Angel. What are you thinking?" He takes my hand and lays it on his chest. Heat spreads through me. I've always been so cold. It's as if my body doesn't waste time on warmth anymore when it needs all the energy to keep my heart beating.

My eyes drop. I'm not sure I can reveal my thoughts. He would be angry with me if I told him. I don't think men do that. Only women who are paid to are willing to touch men like that. A small hint of my depravity is rising to the front of my mind.

I flex my hand and for the first time I feel the warmth of another man's chest. A wave of need drowns out any protest my upbringing might have made, but I don't know how to ask for what I want. How do I ask him to touch me? How do I make him understand that I don't even know what I want? I long to feel his lips on mine again. I yearn to feel his body pressed against mine again. Yet the words stay caught in my throat and all I can do is look up at him.

My desire must show in my eyes because he leans down and presses his lips to mine. His tongue caresses the crease of my lips as if he begs for entrance. I open to him with a groan. His tongue slides inside and strokes my teeth. Unsure of what to do, I leave my hand on his chest. I twist my other hand in the sheets. Blankets cover me and he lies on top of them. The fact that I'm naked skates over the surface of my mind, but I'm too caught up in our kiss to worry about it.

I murmur when he pulls back. I want him to continue kissing me. The firmness of his lips teases me. This is what I need. What I have wanted for so long. Soft, gentle, ladylike kisses don't affect me. I need the scrape of his whiskers across my chin. I want the taste of whiskey and smoke instead of coyly sweet punch.

"Move your mouth. Touch your tongue to mine." He entwines one hand at the back of my head and kisses me again.

I allow him in without hesitation and tease my tongue along his. I don't know if I'm doing what he wants, but he doesn't protest. He sucks on me and my hips arch under the blankets. His free hand slips under the blanket and pinches my nipple. I moan. No one has touched my body aside from myself in years.

Greyson bites my bottom lip and then sucks on it to soothe the sting. He licks a path from my chin to my throat. I press my head back on the pillow and give him more skin to taste. He finds a spot just below my ear and bathes it with his tongue. I move restlessly, unused to the feelings pouring through me. His hand moves from my nipple down to rest low on my stomach. His fingertips pet the curls at the top of my groin. I stiffen and pull away. No other hand has ever touched that spot on my body.

"I'm sorry." I turn my head away, ashamed of my actions. I'm embarrassed that I'm hard and fearful that he will hate me because I don't know what to do.

"No apologies. You're tired. I shouldn't be bothering you." He moves his arm to wrap around my waist and props his head on the palm of his other hand. He doesn't seem angry with me for my inexperience.

"You're not bothering me. I'm not used to this." I gesture to our bodies lying close to each other. "It's not natural to feel good about this."

"Who told you it wasn't natural?"

"My father." I duck my head. A memory flashes through my mind. Father is standing over me, screaming about the perversions found in the joys of the flesh.

"Do you believe him?"

"I have no reason not to." I hesitate. "Yet if it's wrong, why does it feel so good?"

"Because it isn't wrong, Angel. Loving someone—no matter who it is—is never wrong." Greyson sounds like he believes that statement.

"Father is afraid you'll seduce me."

A frown mars his forehead. "Do you want me to leave you alone?"

Here is a decision for me. I have broken away from my father, at least for the moment. I've found a place inside me filled with courage, or maybe it is merely fatalism. If I continue to believe my father, then I've never actually broken out of my cage. Is the flame I feel flickering in my heart courage or desperation? Does it matter?

It doesn't matter if Greyson is trying to seduce me. The outcome will be the same if he just wants to take my innocence. Staring up into his blue eyes, my decision is made. I'll follow wherever this man leads me, even into the places my father fears the most.

I place my hand on his chest over his heart. "Don't leave me. You asked me what I had to lose. I have nothing. I can't lose what I've never had." My gaze drops to the blanket covering me. "I'm empty."

Part Thirteen

"Why do you say that?" He stares at me with a hint of pity in his gaze.

Shrugging, I look down at my hand, lying in my lap. I run my fingers over my wrists. "There's nothing in me. I don't know anything. I'm not smart. I'm empty." I've felt this way for years now. There's a hollow space inside where something might have been, but it's gone and I don't know how to fill it.

"Why does your father hate you?" Greyson wants to understand. I know that's why he's asking these questions.

"I don't know. At first, I thought I made him angry about something, but he continued to beat me. I tried to get him to forgive me. I'd apologize or even beg for his forgiveness. There was nothing." My voice trails off. I'm unsure how to explain my feelings and thoughts.

"He's never told you why he's furious with you?" He takes one of my hands in his. He can't resist touching me. Whenever he is close to me, he seems compelled to caress me in some way.

My pulse leaps when his rough thumb rubs over my scar. "I'm flawed." My whispered words stop his caress for a moment.

"In what way?"

Shutting my eyes, I close myself off from his penetrating gaze. "I'm depraved. Demon spawn. I lust after unnatural passions."

His other hand cups my chin and lifts so that our mouths almost touch. His breath mingles with mine. "What sort of unnatural passions?"

I open my eyes and meet his burning gaze. "I was sixteen before I understood what he meant. I was watching one of the footmen polish some of the family silver. His hands rubbed over and around the object and I found myself getting hard."

My cheeks flush. I can't believe I'm telling him this and yet his touch tells me everything is fine.

"Your prick got hard," he murmurs against my cheek.

I nod. "I wanted him to touch me like he was touching the silver." Shuddering, I remember how much I ached. "My father found me standing and watching. He realized what was happening to me. He started screaming about perversions and how shameful I was. It was then I understood he meant my need for a man to touch me."

"How did he know it wasn't just you being a young man? A stiff breeze could make me randy when I was that age." Greyson's lips nibble along my chin.

"He'd bought me a whore a month before and I couldn't do anything with her. The touch of her hand made me feel dirty. I wanted to run and hide when she put her mouth on me."

I don't say anything about the punishment I received after that episode. Greyson's lips meet mine in a gentle kiss. He sips from my mouth as if he's drinking the finest French wine. My hand tightens on his.

He pulls back enough to whisper, "Did I not just tell you that feeling that way isn't wrong? Passions like that aren't so unnatural that you should be punished for it. I want to show you the joys that can be found in touches like this. You may touch me."

I shake my head. "I don't know where to touch you or how to please you."

"Touch me wherever you wish to or don't touch me at all. I'll not force you into doing something you're not comfortable with." Greyson is sincere. I can tell by the tenderness in his eyes.

I've found the courage to let him kiss me. Now I must find more deep inside me because everything is calling for me to touch him. Taking a breath, I slide my hand into the curls at the base of his neck. My other hand trembles but makes its way around his waist.

He murmurs encouragement against my lips. My fingers find their way under the duke's linen shirt and for the second time in my life, I touch the warm skin of a man. I stroke the small of his back and he shivers. Even though I'm still covered with the blanket, I feel the heat of his body pressing against mine. I want him to lie on me and cover me. I need to soak in his strength.

It might be silly to admit but a thrill of pride races through me. I can make this god tremble. It doesn't matter that my family hates me. For some strange reason this man wants me.

I'm not sure how long we lay kissing and touching. My mind is overwhelmed with sensations and thoughts. My body aches like it did when I was sixteen. Greyson pulls away to lie beside me. He throws one arm over my waist. His golden cheeks are flushed and his breathing ragged. I place my fingers on my swollen lips.

I can't believe how alive I feel. I've never felt the rush of passion or lust before. I whimper.

"What's wrong, love?" He takes my hand and lifts my fingers to his mouth. His slick tongue flicks out and swirls around them.

"I ache."

"Where?" He nibbles at the base of my thumb.

Embarrassment makes me squirm slightly. The gleam in his eyes tells me he knows what he's doing to me. I open my mouth to tell him when a discrete knock sounds on the door.

"Your grace, the Earl is here to see the young lord." A bland voice calls from the hallway.

Greyson sighs and winks. "I'll come down and greet him. Please send Johnson in here," he calls to the servant.

He climbs from the bed and tugs at the front of his pants. My eyes widen at the sight of the bulge his hand touches and a faint smile graces his lips.

"Do I look like a demon to you? I want you, love. It's passion for you that makes me ache, Angel. Just as it's your need for me that makes your shaft throb. Soon you might be willing to let me ease it for you." He heads for the door. "Never hide your true self from me, Angel. With me, you are always safe."

Part Fourteen

I'm still trying to figure out what the duke meant by his last statement when a rather rotund short man dashes into the room.

"He's finally letting me get my hands on you." The man tsks and tries to tug my blankets off.

I hold on to them for dear life. No way would I reveal any part of my body to anyone. I'm not beautiful like Greyson. "Get your hands on me?" That statement would have caused me to cower if anyone but this man had said them. An image of a squirrel rushing around comes to mind and a chuckle pops from my mouth.

"Yes, you poor thing."

Poor thing? Does he know about me? Is he another one who can see all my secrets just by looking at me? I blush and lower my eyes. They say the eyes are the windows to the soul. Maybe my yearning and shame are revealed in them.

The man grabs my hand and pulls me from the bed. I stumble and my embarrassment is complete. Not only am I completely naked but also now my scars are revealed. I hold my hands in front of my manhood and back into the nearest corner.

"I'm suppose to help you get dressed, my lord. His grace told me to." The man bows. "I'm Lord Greyson's valet, Johnson." He doesn't notice my tension.

I shake my head while keeping my eyes fixed on him. "If you can bring me my clothes, I can dress myself." No one had helped me dress since I was ten. My father made anyone who acknowledged me pay.

"Dress yourself? I won't hear of it." Johnson moves closer.

If I weren't so worried about him seeing anything, I would have put my hands out to stop him. Panic starts to well. I try to fight back the blackness swelling around me. I'm going back somewhere I thought I'd left behind.

My eyes move from side to side. I'm trapped. In my heart, I know the valet is only trying to help me. My mind sees his hands reaching for me and I cry out, sliding to the floor. No one except Greyson has ever reached for me without hurting me. My arms cover my head and I wait for the first blow.

"Don't touch me. Please don't hurt me," I beg.

Time slows for me as I curl in the corner. I have no idea how long I've been hiding. A strong hand grips mine. I flinch away. Even though it doesn't let go, the hand doesn't force me to stand.

"Angel, you're safe. Come back from wherever you went."

It's Greyson and I hear the worry in his voice. Peeking over my forearm, I see that we are alone. I throw myself into his arms. I hear my voice, babbling but I can't make out what I'm saying to him.

"Sssh, Angel. It's all right."

"You should have let my father have me back," I whisper against his chest. "I don't know how to live a normal life."

"I will never let your father hurt you again, Angel. It's only been two days. We can't rebuild your world that fast." Greyson sets me back and smiles at me. "This is my fault. I didn't think about Johnson and how you'd react to him."

"My father used to force me to get dressed after he beat me. My shirt would stick to the welts on my back and when I had to undress, he would make his valet tear the fabric away. The pain was horrible. I never let anyone dress me after that." I want to explain. It isn't defiance that makes me refuse his offer. It's the memory of pain.

"Someday I would love to make your father pay for what he's done to you, Angel."

I protest. "You mustn't stand up to Father, your grace. He will destroy you."

He laughs. "Don't worry about me, love. I can handle your father."

A hesitant knock sounds on the door. I press as close to him as I can get. He tells whoever is knocking to come in. Glancing over the duke's shoulder, I watch as Johnson stands just inside the door.

"Your grace, is he okay?"

The concern I hear in the valet's voice surprises me. When my own family doesn't even recognize my existence, a complete stranger's concern for me is odd.

"Yes, Johnson. He's fine now. Bring his clothes in and I'll help him tonight."

"No," I interrupt. I don't want him to see my scars. "I can dress myself. I've been doing so since I was young."

"Johnson, hand me the robe on the bed." Greyson wraps my body in the silk fabric.

I manage to stand. Shame rushes through me. I walk up to Johnson and hold out my hand. He looks at it, then over at Greyson.

"I'm sorry. It wasn't your fault." I must take responsibility for the problems I cause, even if it is just making a servant worry.

Greyson nods and the valet shakes my hand quickly.

"Do you want a bath?" the duke asks.

"No, I'll take one tomorrow. I don't want to cause any more trouble. Is my uncle still here?" I hold myself together by the merest of threads. I really want to climb in bed, cover my head and forget about the world outside.

"Yes, he's waiting downstairs. I'll let him know you'll be down in a few minutes." Greyson kisses my cheek and leaves, herding Johnson out in front of him. He isn't going to let me hide. I have the feeling if I don't go down, the duke would come and get me.

I sit on my bed and pick up the clothes Johnson had laid out for me. The shirt is of the finest linen. The pants are the long pipe-stem style Brummell brought into fashion. I run my hands over the soft golden brocade of the waistcoat. Clothes fit for a prince or a duke. They aren't meant for the likes of me. I want to call out and tell Johnson he's made a mistake, but no one is around to hear me. The lush feeling of the velvet seduces me. I'll wear them down stairs and then explain to Greyson that someone has given me the wrong clothes.

I wonder where these clothes came from. They certainly weren't mine. I've never had anything so nice. I have enough evening clothes for a week of balls, but all the rest of my stuff is barely fit for the rubbish heap. As I stare at these new clothes, I feel something crack inside of me. A door opens in the depths of my soul. Light shines in and I see the possibilities. Maybe I have a chance. Greyson just might be a god with the power to recreate me. I know a new life is there for me if I reach out to take it.

Part Fifteen

Johnson is waiting in the hall for me as I step out of the room. The valet's gaze sweeps over me and I tug on my cuffs. I resist the urge to duck my head in shame.

"Do I look all right?" I'm not sure why I ask but I need assurance. My father would scoff at me for asking a servant their opinion. He believes servants are there to serve and for no other reason.

"You look fine, my lord. His grace wants me to bring you to him and your uncle." Johnson turns and leads me down the hallway.

I wipe my sweating palms on my thighs and follow. My stomach rolls. I don't know why my hands are shaking. My heart pounds and I feel the same as if I were going to face my father's wrath. I'm afraid of what I will find when I join the duke and my uncle.

Fear has always been my constant companion. I fear my father. I've been afraid all my life. As we stop in front of a door on the lower floor, I find my fear changed. I fear Greyson will take one look at me and realize I'm not worth the effort. No one has ever felt that I was worth risking everything for and I fear that's what Greyson is doing by allowing me to stay with him.

If he turns from me, I have nowhere to go. My uncle would offer me a place in his house, but eventually my father would engulf me again. I bite my lip, trying to find the strength to open the door.

"His grace is waiting." Johnson tries to nudge me with his words. He doesn't understand that I know the duke is waiting and that's why I'm having a terrible time getting my feet to move.

A voice deep in my mind tells me I have nothing to lose. If Greyson turns from me, I'd be no worse off than I already am. It is time to start learning how to be normal. Maybe I'm the freak my father claims me to be. Only time will tell if I deserve to live among people, but if I didn't find my own courage, I'll never know the truth. I cringe. *When did I turn into such a sniveling creature?* In the quiet of my mind and the silence of my room, I had been ready to face the tortures of the damned, to be able to step out into the world, but at the first real chance I have, I balk.

I square my shoulders and nod at Johnson. "I'm ready."

The valet stares at me for a moment. He's probably wondering why I took so long. I admit it takes every bit of strength I have to step into the room. Greyson has kissed and touched me. In many ways, he knows me better than anyone else. Yet I'm not confident enough to believe he'll continue to care.

The duke and my uncle look up from where they sit in front of a fireplace. I focus on Greyson because it is his approval I long for. His blue eyes lighten and he stands, holding out a hand to me.

"Angel, I'm glad you've joined us."

Like a child learning to walk, I latch onto his hand for support. "I'm sorry to make you wait," I murmur, nodding a greeting to my uncle.

"It hasn't been that long, son. I'm happy to see you looking better." Uncle's voice is kind.

Greyson gestures to the chair he had been sitting in. I perch on the edge. I know I look as if I'm poised to run but there's a thought that I might need to escape. The duke sits on the arm of the chair, putting his arm on the top behind me. I feel surrounded by him but that's fine with me. I need to know he's near.

Having survived alone for so long, I usually shy away from contact with strangers. Yet from the very beginning, he has invaded my world and become so much more than just a man I'm attracted to. There is an undeniable feeling that he will be here for me when things get bad.

"I wanted to tell you this before you hear it from the gossipmongers," Uncle says. "Your father has been spreading rumors about Greyson brainwashing you. He's saying you're a young innocent child being seduced by an older experienced man. He's trying to gain sympathy by making it seem like the duke is forcing you into being his catamite."

I frown. "What does that mean?" I vaguely remember my father saying the word to Greyson the other night.

"Catamite?" Greyson shifts.

"Yes."

Uncle shares a glance with the duke. Greyson stands and moves to kneel in front of me. He takes my hands in his.

"It is an insult. In Rome, it was used to describe a boy who is the lover of a much older man. Now people use it as a term of ignorance and spitefulness. Your father uses that word to make it look like I'm hurting you or subverting you to do unnatural things. He wants people to believe I'm preying on you. He's trying to make me out to be the villain here. A passion like ours isn't acceptable to many people, Angel."

"Unnatural things? Like kiss and touch?" My eyes are on Greyson. I've forgotten my uncle is in the room with us.

Greyson smiles. "Kissing and touch are part of it. There are other more intimate things we could do and it's those things that your father is talking about."

I flush and my skin warms. My mind doesn't really understand, but there's an instinct in my subconscious that longs to pursue those intimate acts.

Something in me reaches for Greyson and if he wants those shameful things my father is worried about, then I'll give them to him. I'm not sure what love is or how it feels, but if the emotion is anywhere close to what I feel now, I want to continue to explore what we have together. I have a belief forming in my head. Freedom is just around the corner. I'll place my essence in Greyson's hands and let him show me how to discover my true self.

Hidden deep inside the shell I call my body is a soul yearning to find its place in the world. Greyson's gentle hands will lead it out into the light.

Part Sixteen

Uncle coughs, trying to bring our attention back to him. "The other thing I wanted to talk to you about is the fact that I'm going to make you my heir."

I drag my gaze away from the duke as shock races through me. "But why?"

Standing, Greyson keeps a hold of my hand, but turns to look at my uncle. "Are you sure that's a good idea?"

Uncle shrugs and looks away for a moment. "Good or not, it's something I feel I must do."

"To make up for whatever it was you did wrong?" I tighten my grip on the duke's hand. I wonder if this is a dream. If I let go of his hand, will I wake up in my dark room delirious with fever? This seems to be a fantasy created in my fevered mind.

"Yes, it is in a way. One of those I wronged is beyond my reach forever. The other I have never been able to find so that I might rectify my mistake." Uncle's gaze meets mine and I see sadness and shame in his. "But that isn't the only reason why I want to do this for you."

"Williamson has disowned Angel, hasn't he?" Greyson's voice holds outrage and anger.

"Not yet, but if he chooses to stay here with you, my brother won't have any problem trying to erase the young man's existence." Uncle folds his hands and nods at me.

"I don't exist now for him. It doesn't matter to me if I'm his heir or not." I shoot to my feet and start to pace. "I've always assumed he would have Edward take my place." I think about my brother and the few times I'd come in contact with him.

"Edward is your younger brother?" Greyson settles into the chair I vacate.

"Yes. He's Father's favorite child." There is no envy in my

heart for my brother. Being our father's favorite is its own form of torture. Edward's eyes are the same brown and hold the same hopelessness as mine. Yes, there is no joy in being Father's favored son.

"You're probably right, lad. Your father has been making noises for a while now about making Edward his heir instead of you. I think he had a feeling you just might not be as broken as he thought you were." Uncle stands and moves towards the desk in the corner of the room. He picks up a packet of papers. Waving me over, he hands them to me. "Look these over. Take your time and let me know how you feel later."

I stare down at the brown string wrapped around the papers. Who knew life could change with the untying of such a small piece of twine? I nod because there's nothing else I can say at the moment. I don't know if I can accept this. I never thought I'd have anything except emptiness for the rest of my life.

"If you'd like, I can have my solicitor look over the papers for you, Angel," Greyson offers from his place across the room.

"Thank you, your grace." I smile slightly at my uncle. "I thought my father was your heir, Uncle."

"He would be if my title was entailed the normal way, but somehow the first Earl managed to keep control of who the title went to. I can make any male my heir. He doesn't even have to be related to me, if that's the way I want it." Uncle's hand grips my shoulder and he squeezes. "Don't worry. You'll be a good Earl."

I shrug, unsure of all of this. What do I know about running an estate? I can't take care of myself. How will I be able to manage other people's lives? I watch my uncle say goodbye to the duke. Greyson escorts him out and I walk to the window. It overlooks a small garden with a fountain in the middle. I don't fight the urge and I find the doors leading out onto a veranda. Stepping outside, I wander down to the fountain. I stare into the cascading water and let my mind go blank.

Strong arms wrap around my waist and I'm pulled against Greyson's chest. I know it's him by the familiar scent filling my nose. In an instant, I relax and allow his strength to support me. As with our first encounter, the darkness hides reality and I can pretend for a moment that I am normal.

"What are you thinking?" His voice bathes my ear in warmth.

"This is all a dream. In a minute, I'll wake up in my cold bedroom and Father will be yelling at me for something I didn't even know I did." I want to add that good things like this don't happen to me.

"Is that why you haven't fallen apart yet? You still believe this is all a dream?" One of Greyson's hands moves up to slide under my waistcoat and rest against my chest. I know he can feel the pounding of my heart. His other hand lies just above my groin and my shaft hardens.

The tone of my laugh is hysterical. "I'm holding on by my fingertips, your grace."

"Greyson," he murmurs as his lips brush my neck.

"What?" I'm distracted by the light sweep of his fingers over the front of my pants.

"Please call me Greyson. I don't want formality from you. I hope we've moved beyond that." His teeth scrape a spot beneath my ear, bringing a gasp to my lips.

"Greyson." His name is a whisper as I lean my head to the side and offer him more of my skin. "It must be a dream. No one touches me anymore. No one cares enough to offer me protection."

"I will protect you forever, Angel, if you will only trust me." Urgency holds court in his words even as his teeth nibble on my ear. I place my right hand over his hand that shields my heart. I find the courage to cover his other hand with mine and press it tighter to the bulge in my pants.

I want to explain that I do trust him. I trust him more than I have ever trusted anyone. I have deserted my father for him. I have opened myself up to disappointment and hurt because of this man holding me so carefully in his arms. He is a stranger yet

I give him my very life to do whatever he will with it because in his eyes I see the man I can become.

Part Seventeen

Taking a deep breath, I turn in his arms and cradle his face in my hands. I stare up at his blue eyes. In their depths I see an emotion that causes me to tremble. I don't have a name for it, but it makes me feel safe and cared for. My tongue wets my lips and he moans.

I do that to him. I can make him moan and shiver. I bring his head down, pressing our lips together. He doesn't try to take control of the kiss even though I'm not sure of what I'm doing. I bite his bottom lip, then lick it to soothe the sting. He opens for me and I slide my tongue inside to stoke the roof of his mouth right behind his teeth. A shudder wracks his body.

His arms encircle my waist, bringing our bodies together. Yet he moves with caution as if to give me a chance to protest or stop him. I won't stop him. Not this time. Though I have no idea what to do, I'm willing to let him show me.

My father's voice snarls in my head, telling me I should be ashamed. The emotions I'm feeling from the touch of his mouth and the brush of his hands are wrong and will send me straight to Hell. I push the words to the back of my mind and ignore them. For the first time in my life, I'm taking something I want, and what I want is Greyson.

His hands cup my buttocks and tighten a little. I moan at the strength of his firm grip. His tongue invades my mouth and he slowly starts taking control of our kiss. I try to keep my eyes open and focus on his. I want to see the passion rise in them as it has the few times we've touched, but desire is overwhelming me as our pricks brush against each other.

Greyson rocks our hips together while his lips trail down my cheek to my neck. "Wrap your leg around me," he whispers in my ear.

I do as he tells me. I'm not worried about falling. He'll support me even if my own legs fail me. Our new position brings our groins tighter together and I gasp as lust rushes through me. All I can think of is getting closer to him.

The duke encourages me to rub against him. Pressure builds. My shaft aches. I don't know what is happening. I whimper. Greyson surrounds me. One hand is on my backside. The other slips between us and cradles my aching prick.

I'm rubbing. He's stroking. The tingle grows at the base of my spine. An explosion is building, but I'm afraid to release it. I fear I'll shatter into a million pieces and won't be able to put myself back together.

"Open your eyes, Angel. Look at me," Greyson orders.

I force my heavy eyelids open, so I can focus on his gaze. Understanding mingles with desire, making his blue eyes glitter. Another emotion hides amidst those two. It's one I've seen in his glance before but I have no name for it.

"You'll catch me?" I'm hanging over a cliff, needing his assurance before I let go.

"Let go. I promise I'll catch you." He leans down and scrapes his teeth over my skin above my collar.

The sting of his bite combines with the rough pressure of his hand and I give in. My muscles tense. My back arches and I cry out. It feels as if I'm releasing my soul.

Greyson's hand continues to stroke me with each jerk of my hips. I feel his lips moving against my neck, but I don't know what he's saying. My vision begins to blur and I black out.

When I open my eyes, I'm curled on his lap and we're sitting on the edge of the fountain. One of his arms wraps around my waist. The other cradles me against his chest. His lips brush my hair and his breathing is ragged.

I lean back to look into his eyes. "Are you all right?"

He smiles and nods. "I'm fine. How are you?"

"Tired." I blink, resisting the urge to snuggle close and go to sleep.

Laughing, he hugs me close. "I'm feeling tired myself. Let's go to bed before my servants come out and find us sleeping in the garden."

At the mention of his servants, I stiffen. "What will they say about us?" I'm thinking about the kiss Greyson gave me in front of Johnson. I wonder what the valet thought of me throwing my naked body into the duke's arms.

"They know about my taste in bed partners, Angel. They won't say anything. If any of them treat you disrespectfully, tell me. I'll deal with them." His voice is firm and confident.

"My father's servants ignore me. It makes their lives easier." I grimace, remembering what happened to the last servant who was kind to me.

"My servants work for me out of loyalty and respect. They don't fear me. Trust me. You above all others will be treated as an honored guest." He stands, still holding me in his arms.

I find I don't mind being carried like a child. "What happened to me back there?"

"You really are an innocent." He chuckles.

Blushing, I lay my head on his shoulder to hide my embarrassment.

"I'm not making fun of you, dear one. What you experienced is pleasure. Your body enjoyed what we were doing so much that you spilled your seed."

The front of my trousers is wet and I wrinkle my nose in disgust.

"Did you enjoy it?" The laughter leaves Greyson's voice and I know I must tell him the truth.

"Yes, I did." It is a simple statement that barely covers the surface of how I felt at the moment of my spending, and how I feel as he carries me into the house.

Part Eighteen

Greyson grins at me as he makes his way up the stairs. "That's just the beginning of what I want to teach you, Angel. There is much pleasure to be found in loving each other."

"More pleasure?" I'm not sure what to think about that. I had enjoyed what we did out in the garden so much, I think my mind would stop functioning if it had been even more pleasurable. "And you'll show me?"

He pushes open the door to his room and carries me inside. He keeps a firm grip on my shoulders as he lowers my feet to the floor. "If you want me to, I'll show you everything I know. I'll teach you to love me."

I wrap my arms around his waist and press my nose against his throat. In the short time I've been with the duke, his scent has come to mean safety to me. After never feeling safe in my own home, it is a relief to know he'll take care of me if I need him.

"Why me?" I can't get my mouth to tell him I already love him. I have loved since the first moment I saw him in the ballroom that night.

"Before I answer, we should get ready to go to bed. We'll be more comfortable there." He pulls away from and starts to unbutton my waistcoat.

I squeak. Except for earlier in the night, I had never been naked in front of anyone. His hands falter and he stares at me with disappointment in his eyes. I hate having put that emotion on his face.

"Of course, you might not wish to share my bed. I'm sorry. Again I'm forcing you." He steps away.

"I want to share your bed. I don't feel truly safe unless you're with me." I glanced at my trembling hands. My scars peek out from under my cuffs. "I'm scarred."

Greyson takes my hands and bares my wrists to the light. "I

know. I've seen them. They don't matter to me, Angel. I have marks of my own."

Shaking my head, I tug my hands free. I wonder if I'm testing the duke. Showing him the outward signs of my depravity to see if he'll turn from me. The time has come to reveal all of myself to him and shed the last chains from my soul.

I strip off my waistcoat and let it drop to the floor. My hands shake so badly, I struggle to untie my cravat and get my shirt off. I can tell he wants to help me, but I shake my head. This is something I must do for myself.

"Don't. Not if it hurts you this much," Greyson protests, holding his hands out to me.

I don't know I'm crying until a tear drops on to my hand. It almost seems to burn as it slides off. I move to where the light from the candles baths me in a soft glow. Closing my eyes, I turn until I'm facing away from him and my back is bared to him in all its mutilated glory.

I don't hear anything. It's as if Greyson has stopped breathing. I hesitate, but then force myself to glance over my shoulder. His face holds no expression. His blue gaze traces each of my scars and it feels as if he's burning me. Anger flares in his eyes.

"Monster," he spits out the word and it drives like a dagger into my heart.

What I fear has come true. He thinks I'm a monster. A freak. I should never have stepped beyond my cage. Tears blind me and I try to find my shirt without letting him know how his words have wounded me.

"I'm so sorry," I whisper. I clutch the fine linen shirt to my chest and turn to face him.

"Sorry for what?" He frowns.

What am I sorry for? Living? Breathing? For coming into his world and trying to prove I have the right to be there? So many things I want to apologize for, but all I can say is, "I'm sorry for my scars."

"No, don't be sorry for those. They aren't your fault." He reaches for me.

I try to move away from him. "You called me a monster." I tremble, wishing his words didn't hurt so much. I should be used to insults and yet his words cut so deep I thought blood should be dripping from my chest.

He takes me in his arms and pulls me to his chest. His hands rest lightly on my back as if he's afraid to hold me too tight. "No Angel. Love, I was calling your father a monster. You're not a monster. You're so innocent and beautiful. Your scars only help to convince me of your strength."

"Strength? What strength?" I push away from him and pace to the other side of the room. "I look at them and see fear. I see cowardice. I see them as the branding of a freak."

"Don't call yourself that. Never insult the man I love like that." His voice is fierce and I blink in surprise.

Greyson's words shock me. He has called me "love" a few times and I figured it was just a common endearment he used with everyone. But here he is saying that he loves me. I drop to my knees and bury my face in my hands. Sobs tears through me. He kneels beside me and wraps me in his arms while murmuring words of love to me. Our tears mix together.

Finally, I'm tired. Tired of crying. Tired of feeling like I need to apologize for who I am. I set back on my heels and stare at him. His blue eyes are concerned, but there's no disgust in his face for me. There's only acceptance and love. I have a name for the emotion I've seen in his expression and have heard in his voice.

Greyson loves me. Me, the Angel he's trying to rescue from Hell.

Part Nineteen

He lifts me to my feet and unbuttons my trousers with slow fingers. I'm not inclined to stop this beautiful golden man with sky blue eyes. I can't quit staring at his face. His cheeks are rough as I slide my hand over his skin. I shiver as I imagine the stubble rubbing over my stomach.

"I should shave," he comments while turning to press a kiss into my palm.

"Why?" I'm not really paying attention to his words. My mind is focusing on the fact that he's slipping his hand into my trousers. There's only a thin layer of cotton between his warmth and my prick.

"I don't want to mark your skin." He squeezes his hand around my shaft.

"Uh." I can't seem to think or even worry about what he might do to me. "I won't mind."

He chuckles and strokes his hand over me. Groaning, I push against him. He squeezes me again and then tugs my trousers down to my feet. He kneels and I stare down at him. Never would I have thought one of the most powerful me in all of England would be kneeling at my feet as if worshipping me. I choke back a laugh. He isn't worshipping me. He's trying to get my shoes off.

Resting my hand on his shoulder, I let him undress me and within seconds, I'm naked. Nervousness causes a chill to flood my skin. I'm not comfortable having him stare at me, but I know he won't laugh at me. He stands and cups my cheek. I turn my face and place a kiss on his palm.

Taking my hand, Greyson leads me to his bed. I climb in and slide under the covers. I feel my eyes widen and my mouth falls open as I watch Greyson undress. I've never seen a naked man, but something tells me that he is an unusual specimen.

He joins me in the bed and I can't help but reach out to trail my hand over his chest. The tips of my fingers tangle in the light hair covering the muscles. I graze a fingernail over the nub of flesh and Greyson groans.

"I don't have hair there." I'm fascinated by the hair that tickles my palms as I run down the thin line heading down to his groin. His prick rises from a nest of coarse dark blond curls. I look at him while my hand hangs over him.

Smiling at me, he takes my hand in his and engulfs his shaft. "Touch me, Angel. I've imagined it for so long."

I'm not sure what I should be doing. How does he want me to touch him? Do I stroke him hard or with a gentle touch? I've never even touched myself like I'm holding him now. "I don't know how."

"We have all night. There's no hurry, love. Let me show you." He guided my hand up and down in a tight stroke.

His prick throbs against my fingers. It feels like silk over steel and my own shaft fills. I don't notice when his hand leaves me. His foreskin pulls back and reveals the glistening head of his prick. I run my thumb over the wet head and tease the leaking slit. Greyson groans and thrusts his hips, moving with increasing force and speed.

"Will you let me show you something?" His voice is harsh and labored, but I think it's from pleasure.

"Yes." I'm willing to let him show me anything.

"I won't hurt you." He pushes against my shoulder and soon I'm lying on my back, staring up at him.

"I know." As much as I know he won't hurt me, I can't help but stiffen as his hand cups my prick. No one else has ever touched me there.

He presses his lips to my mouth. His thumb teases the slit in the head of my cock, swiping the liquid welling from it and spreading it around my skin. He slides his tongue inside and strokes the sensitive roof of my mouth. I moan and shift under him. His rough palm cups my sac and rolls them in his fingers. I feel a light touch to the skin behind my balls and I cry out.

"Greyson," I moan, gripping his arms tight as the pleasure begins to build in me.

"Hold on, love." He moves away from me to reach for a small jar sitting on the stand next to the bed.

I jerk as cool slick fingers grip my shaft and start stroking with tight movements. I arch my back and begin to beg with my hips for him to move faster. He understands my silent pleas. When the cool fingers of his other hand touch me in my most private of areas, I freeze.

"Sh, love. Trust me. There will be a little pressure and maybe a little pain, but I promise you'll enjoy it when you relax."

I stare up at him. All I see in his blue eyes is love and caring. He hasn't lied to me yet. He believes that I will enjoy what he wants to do to me. Taking a deep breath, I manage to relax. He taps my thigh and I spread my legs even more, so he can fit between them. A fingertip glides over my opening and I shiver. He brushes a kiss over my cheek, calming me as a finger breeches my hole.

"Ah," I gasp and arch. The sensation is strange. There's pressure and a slight pain, but when he pulls the tip out and presses back in, a burst of pleasure rushes through me.

I'm not sure how far in he goes this time, but I feel full. He twists his finger and rubs against a spot that makes me cry out as sparks shoot through my body.

"Please." I have no idea what I'm begging for, but Greyson does.

More pressure fills me and I moan, spreading my legs farther apart. Soon I'm swimming in sensations. I'm caught between his fingers moving inside me and his mouth tasting my neck.

Suddenly the fingers leave and I protest. Greyson covers me, placing his hands on each side of my shoulders. His blue eyes stare down at me as a bigger pressure begins to fill me. I whimper as the pain burns through the pleasure.

"Breathe, love." Greyson stops and lets me get used to what he's doing.

I breathe and push up on my elbows to stare down at our groins. I glance at Greyson in shock. His prick is inside me. I didn't know this was possible. He kisses me with gentle lips and starts pushing farther into me. Within a minute, he is buried as deep as he can get and I'm forgetting the pain. Pleasure rushes through me as he rubs over that same spot he'd hit with his fingers.

"You're perfect, love."

We rock together and his stomach strokes over my prick. The same feeling I had out in the garden builds in me. It pools at the base of my spine. I wrap my arms and legs around Greyson's body. Instinct takes over and I encourage him to continue.

Passion rips through me and I throw my head back, feeling my seed spill over my stomach. As my eyes drift close, I see Greyson cry out and a wet heat fills me. I black out again.

When I come back to myself, Greyson is cuddled close to me and I'm clean. Exhaustion drags me back down, but not before I kiss the duke.

"Thank you," I whisper against his chest over his heart.

"For what?" Greyson runs his hand down my back.

"For loving me." My eyes close.

"I'll love you forever if you let me." Greyson murmurs and presses a kiss to my cheek.

Part Twenty

I open my eyes to see the early morning sun shine through the crack in the curtains. My body aches in odd places and I find myself blushing as I think of what Greyson and I did last night. He promised to show me pleasure and he did.

The way he touched me last night. How full I felt when he slid his prick into me. All those things race through my mind. I'm waiting for my father's voice to berate me. I'm waiting for the shame to hit and the tears to fall. Yet I can't feel ashamed of what we did. Not now. At some point, I know I'll be shocked and upset because of how wrong it is for us to love each other that way, but right now, it feels perfect and right.

Is it right because Greyson says he loves me? I frown. Has the perversion hiding in my soul tainted our love? My hands shake. What if he has changed his mind? No matter what he tells me in the darkness of night, how can he feel the same when sunlight shows the truth? Light reveals the flawed creature I am. I long for him to take me in his arms and tell me everything is okay.

I turn to face his side of the bed. It's empty. He's gone and my heart breaks a little. Fear claws its way into my mind. I know it can't be too late in the morning. I don't sleep in because the earlier I get up, the more likely I am to have an hour or so of freedom. Where did he go this early in the morning? Someone knocks quietly on the door.

"Come in," I call, making sure I'm covered. Maybe someday I'll be comfortable in my own skin, but for now, I hide.

"Good morning, my lord." Johnson bustles in. "I hope you slept well."

My cheeks heat and I know I'm blushing again. "I slept fine, Johnson. Where is Greyson?"

"His Grace had some business to take care of at the Home Office. You'll find he's often called there to give advice." Johnson makes his way to the windows.

Relief rushes through me. Greyson didn't leave me because he's disgusted with my ignorance. He's at the Home Office. Pride hits me. The prime minister asks my love for advice.

Johnson pulls open the curtains and then goes to the wardrobe. "His Grace said to let you know that you may have breakfast in bed or downstairs. Whichever is comfortable for you."

I watch for a moment as Johnson sets a pile of clothes on the chair nearest the bed. A pitcher of hot water, a bowl and a towel is placed on the dresser. The valet turns to look at me, waiting for my answer.

"I'll eat downstairs. No sense in making more work for you." I glance out the window at the sunny day. "If I were home, I'd sneak out and go riding, but my horse isn't here. I hope Father doesn't harm him." It's something my father would do. I'm out of his reach, so he'll take his anger out on an innocent creature that can't fight back.

"A young stable boy showed up earlier this morning leading a horse. The lad wore your father's livery. He explained that the horse was yours and you must have forgotten to get him when you left." Johnson winks at me.

I'm puzzled by who would send my horse to me, since fearing my father's wrath, the servants chose to ignore me. "If I may, I'd like to go for a ride."

"My lord, you can do whatever you want. I have your riding clothes ready. While you're getting dressed, I'll inform the stable to have your mount saddled and waiting outside for you." Johnson bows and leaves.

It still surprises me that I don't have to ask for permission here. I climb out of bed, eager to go riding and feel the taste of freedom again. I stop in the middle of washing when I realize I'm not held captive here against my will. If I chose to, I can walk away. Greyson won't hold me. I know now it would hurt him if I left, but he'd cheer me on even while he cried.

In so many ways, I'm free from the cage I'd lived in all my

life, but I'm also held captive here by something deeper than shame. It's an emotion stronger than fear. The chains holding me here are made of the softest velvet yet are harder to break than iron. I'm bound to Greyson by love and this is a restraint I gladly accept.

I race downstairs where Greyson's butler directs me to a small breakfast room. A single plate is placed at one end of the table with steaming eggs and bacon on it. I try not to gobble the food, but I'm starving, which is unusual for me. I've gone days without eating before, especially after my father has expressed his disappointment in me. Today though, I find joy in the chewing and swallowing of the food. Setting the silverware down, I bound to my feet and toss my napkin on the table.

"Tell the cook it was wonderful," I call as I race from the room towards the front door.

Johnson is waiting for me with my coat, hat and gloves. I'm bouncing on the balls of my feet as I tug my gloves on. For the first time, I'm excited about facing the day. I'm interested in what is going on outside the door. Could one night of loving change everything about me? Or am I finally finding the thrill of living I'd never known existed?

"Have a good ride, my lord." Johnson opens the door and gestures to where my gelding is waiting for me.

"Thank you, Johnson. If Greyson gets back before I do, tell him where I went." I throw myself into the saddle and take off.

Johnson's words drift after me. "He'll know where you are."

Part Twenty-One

Greyson is home when I return from my ride. I hand the butler my hat and gloves. Without taking my eyes off the golden god walking towards me, I allow the butler to help me off with my coat. As soon as I'm free, I move to meet Greyson in the hallway.

He brushes a finger over my cheek and smiles. "Enjoy your ride, love?"

"Yes, I did. I'm surprised Jack managed to get my gelding out of the stable without Father knowing about it." I reach out and touch his arm, convincing myself he's real and with me.

"Well, if he hadn't, I would have bought you a mount. I remember how happy you looked riding in the Park." He takes my hand and leads me down the hall to the study where we met my uncle last night. "I thought I'd find you still asleep. You aren't too sore from last night?"

Heat blossoms in my face and I duck my head, embarrassed by his frankness. My prick hardens as well, merely from the touch of his hand and his scent filling my nose.

"You blush just like a maiden." His hands cup my face and lifts my gaze to meet his. "I don't mean to make you uncomfortable, Angel. I'm a little unsure how to treat you. I'm not used to dealing with one so innocent."

I see the worry and concern in his eyes. He is worried about scaring me or embarrassing me. I don't think he's been nervous or unsure of himself in decades. I place my hands over his and press them closer to my skin.

"Don't treat me like a fragile creature about to break. As you've said yourself, I'm stronger than I look. I just need time to adjust. I've never been in any kind of relationship—friendship or whatever it is we have here. All my life, I've heard that everything we did last night was wrong and depraved. Though I'll admit I had no idea men could do that. My father never went into details about those acts he called perversions." I kiss the palms of each hand and hold one to my chest over the spot where my heart beats.

"I'm sure your father wouldn't know exactly what we do either. He's one of many who would claim any sort of passion and love to be wrong." He mimics my action and my hand rests over his heart.

The beat is strong and true. I have the feeling that his heart beats for me now and were I to leave, it would stop. I stare up at him, not understanding how I got to be so lucky. Is God smiling at me to make this man fall in love with me? We step closer to each other.

"Why?" It's the question repeating over and over in my mind, though I'm less concerned about the answer now.

"I'll tell you, but come and sit with me."

I follow him to the chair I sat in last night. He sits and tugs me down onto his lap. I curl up, resting my head on his shoulder. His arms wrap around me. I'm safe and warm. Love swells through me. Nothing must happen to the man because of me. Fear tries to raise its ugly head. I know my father won't give up. He'll try to tear us apart. Are the chains we are forging between each other going to be strong enough to withstand his assault?

Greyson's hand trails over my arm and rests on my hip. "Do you know when I saw you for the first time?"

"Was it the ball where you kissed me?" That was when I first noticed him.

"No. That was the night I finally saw my interest returned. Which is why I followed you out into the garden and kissed you." He laughed softly. "I must be better at sulking and spying than I thought."

"I'm sure you're marvelous at spying, but I wouldn't have noticed you before then. I was too caught up in my own misery. That night was the first night I wasn't in pain from Father's abuse." I gasp as his arms tighten around me.

"I would call him out if I could." Anger causes his voice to become a growl.

I stroke my hand over his arm. "I know, but he isn't worth the chance of you getting injured in some way. I'm free of him now. So when was the first time you saw me?" I want to distract him away from his anger at my father.

"It was at the first ball of the Season. I planned on just making an appearance and then leaving. I don't spend a great deal of time in Society. The people try my patience. I went because my friend's wife was giving the ball and it would make her happy if the Duke of Northampton showed." Greyson sounds annoyed.

"I went to that one because my father made me. He forced me out of bed and dressed me. He told me I needed to make an appearance. I thought about protesting, but my back still wore the marks from my last beating. So I went." I remember that night. I had been in such a haze of pain, I wouldn't have noticed the regent if he'd been standing in front of me. Though I remember the man standing on the veranda while I hid in the darkness.

"That explains why you were so pale and your eyes so sad. I walked in and there you were. It was as if a light shone down on you and a voice spoke in my ear as clearly as you are talking to me." Awe fills his voice.

"What did it say?"

"You were the one. The one I'd been searching for all of my life." Greyson sighs and nods towards the portrait of his wife on the wall above the mantel. "I married my wife when I was twenty-two. Our fathers arranged our marriage. I knew I needed to have an heir. I didn't have the strength to say no. I knew I could never love her."

"Were you faithful to her?" I'm not sure why I want to know.

"Yes, I was." He hugs me closer to him. "I never shared anyone's bed, not even hers after our second son was born. I was celibate for twelve years and then she died. I found myself free from the constraints of my marriage and Society. I had my heir and the title now. Yet I wasn't happy. I came to Town looking for something, but I didn't know what until the night I saw you. I never believed in love at first sight, yet when I saw you, I knew I would love you."

The honesty in his voice tells me he believes what he is saying. How anyone could know they would love me just from seeing me once confuses me. I don't think of myself as lovable.

"I turned to ask one of my friends who you were. When I tried to point you out to him, you were gone. I went outside, but I couldn't find you and no one I asked knew who you were. I kept my inquiries contained to my closest friends. None of the gossipmongers needed to know I was interested in you. Finally one of them told me you were Williamson's heir. By then all I knew was you were my Angel and all the rest of it was just nonsense. I held my breath in anticipation whenever I went to a ball. Would you be there? Would I get a chance to talk to you? Your eyes brought tears to mine. You were so sad. So lonely. Then I followed you into the garden and lost my heart completely." He looks into my eyes and smiles. "I don't want you to live a lie like I had to. You deserve to be given a chance to live as honestly as possible. Even if you decide to leave me, I want to give you the confidence to live. I never had anyone to support me when I needed it. I'll protect you and keep you safe until you don't need me anymore."

He lifts my chin and presses a gentle kiss to my lips. I let him in, wrapping my arms around his neck and moving as close as I can to him. The first kiss we shared, the one he said caused him to lose his heart, was the one to hand me the key to my freedom. I want to explain how our kiss made me understand I was worth something more than just being a whipping boy. I want to explain that there might be the possibility that I'll always need him. But I don't want to stop kissing him long enough to tell him. It can wait.

Part Twenty-Two

His hands bury themselves in my hair and he tilts my head to deepen the kiss. I nibble on his bottom lip and then bathe the sting away with my tongue. I end up on my knees, straddling his legs. I rock my hips, rubbing our pricks together. Even through our clothes, I shiver from the contact. One of his hands drops to cup my buttocks and presses our bodies tight together.

"Oh," is all I can say. Sensation races over my skin. His mouth trails down my neck and he sucks at a tender spot beneath my ear. It feels like the spot is connected directly to my prick. With each suck my hips jerk. We both groan.

A discrete cough interrupts our kisses. I start to hide my face in Greyson's chest. But his finger under my chin stops me. I meet his eyes and he smiles at me.

"No more hiding, love. In this house, you're safe." Greyson brushes another kiss over my lips. I take a deep breath as I nod. He eases me off his lap and helps me stand. Ignoring whoever stands behind me, he hugs me close. I soak in his warmth and hold his love tight to my heart.

We turn to see the butler standing just inside the room. He gestures towards the study. Greyson nods and smile down at me.

"Come with me." His arm encircles my waist and he escorts me to the other room.

When we enter the study, there is a stranger sitting at Greyson's desk. The duke laughs and holds out a hand to the man.

"Roberts, I'm going to send this desk to your office. You use it more than I do."

Roberts stands and shakes the duke's hand. Turning, he offers me his hand as well. I stare at it. No one had ever acknowledged me without being forced to.

"Angel, this is Roberts. He's my solicitor and I had him go over the papers your uncle brought over. Roberts, this is my

Angel." Greyson introduces us.

I shake his hand and hope he doesn't notice how sweaty my palm is.

"I've checked everything and it looks all in order. Your uncle has the right to name any male his heir. It's now up to you and what you wish to do." Roberts must see my shock because he taps my hand with a finger. "You don't have to make a decision at this moment or even in the next week. There is time."

"Thank you." It's the only thing I can think of to say. I never thought I'd be heir to my uncle's title. To be honest, I didn't believe I'd live to be my father's heir. There were moments when I thought my father would kill me, but no more. Suddenly I have the chance to become an Earl.

"Your Grace, I have some papers I need to go over with you." Roberts points to the desk.

"Of course." Greyson heads to the desk.

I don't know what to do. I don't want to listen in on the duke's private business. I move towards the door. Greyson looks up.

"You don't have to leave, love. I don't have any secrets from you." Greyson gestures for me to come back to him.

I shake my head. "I think I'll go upstairs and clean up."

He studies me as if he isn't sure about letting me go.

"I'm fine. I just need to be alone for a while. Things have changed and I need to think about them." I smile to reassure him.

"Fine. Come back down when you're finished." He looks back down at the papers Roberts sets in front of him.

Johnson is waiting in the hall for me as I leave the room. The valet follows me up the stairs after telling the footmen to bring hot water up for a bath. It's still morning, but I need to change and clean up. It's my way of washing away my old life and starting a new one.

Thirty minutes later, I sink into the warm water. In the course of four hours, my life has changed a great deal. Someone loves me enough to give me new opportunities and a new world. He trusts me even though we've only just met. I scrub my body, and the marks Greyson left on my skin last night make me blush.

For the first time I've felt passion. I've enjoyed another person's touch. I've tasted someone else's lips. I've found Heaven with a golden god. Our relationship is one Society considers depraved, but it is one I've never known before. Greyson accepts me and loves me no matter what I've done.

I glance around the room. Dark wood forms the bed and the furniture that speaks to the masculinity of the man who sleeps there. I see the tall, muscular blond man whose golden looks caught my eye. In the blue of the silk bed cover, I see his piercing gaze. Yet sitting on the dresser is a small jade statue of an elephant, speaking of a certain whimsy in him.

I rest my head back against a rolled towel and close my eyes. Two nights ago, I was nothing; just a scapegoat for my father to abuse. In the blink of an eye, I am someone's love. I'm first in line to one of the oldest earldoms in the country. My father is going to disown me, but I seem to have found a different family. A family that accepts me for what and who I am. While I'm not entirely sure of my uncle, I'd trust Greyson with my life.

A hand caresses my chest, teasing my nipples. I gasp and a mouth pressing against my lips takes my breath. Opening my eyes, I look up into those blazing blue eyes as his tongue duels with mine. I acknowledge to myself that nothing else means anything to me except the love of this man.

Part Twenty-Three

His rough fingers pluck at my nipples and I lift my chest, offering him more of my skin to play with. His mouth trails over my chin to find the spot he had sucked on earlier.

"Please." I beg for his touch.

His other hand slides down my chest and under the water to cup my prick. My hips rock up, thrusting me through his palm. The firmness of his grip makes me moan. His thumb swipes over the crown of my shaft and pushes into the opening. There's a little burst of pain and I hiss. Greyson stills.

"Are you okay?" He pulls away from me to check

"Yes." I nod.

"I didn't hurt you, did I?" He stands and holds his hands out to me.

Taking a hold of him, I allow him to pull me to my feet. The warm water slides off my skin. His hot gaze burns me as his eyes trace a path from my face down my chest to where my shaft rises from its nest of curls.

"No," I manage to answer. "You didn't hurt me." After the cutting lash of my father's whip, it would take more than Greyson's touch to hurt me. I step from the tub and reach for the towel Johnson had left on the chair.

Greyson grabs it before me. He takes his time drying my arms and chest. I want to yank the fabric from him and insist that I can take care of myself, but there is something in his eyes that tells me he wants to do this for me and at the moment, I'm willing to let him. He kneels at my feet and starts to dry my legs. I play with the blond curls on his head, running my fingers through them. I can't get over the fact that he allows me to touch him. No one in my life before this would let me touch them. Maybe they were afraid my disease would rub off on them.

He tosses the towel behind him and grins up at me. "You said you felt dirty when the woman tried to put her mouth on you. How would you feel if I did it?"

Shock races through me. I didn't know men would want to do that. I admit to myself there are a lot of things I don't know. Greyson must realize that I'm struck speechless because he leans forward and wraps his lips around the head of my prick. Pleasure rushes through me and my knees buckle. His hands take a firm grip on my buttocks and he supports me as he takes my shaft deeper into the moist heat of his mouth.

I grasp his shoulder while entwining my fingers in the curls at the back of his head. My chin rests on my chest as I stare down at him. His sparkling blue eyes meet mine without shame and I understand that he's getting as much pleasure out of this as I am. He increases the pressure as he slowly pulls back until just the tip rests in his mouth. I jump when his tongue teases the slit in the head, tasting the drops of my seed leaking out. He hums and the vibration causes shivers to trace through my body.

His hands teach my hips how to move. Does he really want me to push my shaft in and out of his mouth? I try to resist, but he's stronger than I am, so I begin to thrust. Now that his shoulder supports me, his hands glide across my body to find places that make my passion build.

"Greyson," I moan as the fingers of one hand tap my opening. His other hand makes its way between my legs and strokes the skin there. I widen my stance and grip his shoulder tighter.

The finger pushing into my opening forces a gasp out of my mouth. He encourages me to rock between his finger and mouth. Sensations pool at the base of my spine. I can no longer think, only move. His tongue bathes the underside of my shaft as he swallows me down until I hit the back of his throat. The muscles in his throat massage me and I am helpless to do anything except move as he insists.

One deep thrust of his finger and he hits the spot that causes my eyesight to cloud and my body to tense. "God," I cry out. Pressure builds and I can tell my soul longs for release.

Another thrust and rub against that spot. I arch my back, shoving my shaft deep into Greyson's mouth. My seed spills from me and my muscles stiffen. All I can think of is the pleasure rolling through me. My mind blacks out.

When I regain my senses, I find I'm lying on the bed, covered by a sheet. Greyson is slowly stripping his clothes off. I shift and he turns to smile at me. The sudden need to share with him all the joy he brings me hits and I reach for him.

"Please let me give you the same pleasure," I beg.

He laughs softly and shakes his head. "Tonight, you may do whatever you wish to me, Angel. Right now, I'm fine. I spilled my seed when you did. You're so beautiful."

Blushing, I hide my face. I don't see the beauty in me, but I won't argue with him. I watch as he washes and then pulls on the bell cord. Climbing in bed, he cradles me close to him. A knock sounds on the door. Johnson pokes his head in.

"Have lunch ready in two hours, Johnson." Greyson doesn't look at the valet. He buries his face against my neck.

"Certainly, your Grace." Johnson nods and shuts the door.

My eyes want to shut and I fight for a few minutes. Sleeping in the middle of the day isn't something I've ever been allowed to do. Greyson's arms encircle me and his hands stroke my back.

"Relax, love. Sleep and when we get up, we'll go to my tailor's for some more clothes for you." His voice bathes my ear.

"I don't want you to be paying for me. I shouldn't take anything from you when I haven't earned any of it." My breathing falls into the same rhythm as his.

"Your uncle is providing you with an allowance like he would with any heir. Maybe he'll give you a little extra and Roberts can show you how to invest it. You can have your own money without relying on anyone, not even me." He understands and isn't angry with my refusal.

Money of my own. If I had that, then if there comes a time when I must leave Greyson to save him, I'd be able to survive for a while on my own. A chill wracks my body and he holds me closer to him, throwing one of his legs over my thigh and surrounding me with his warmth. I don't ever want to leave him. I know I'll fight as hard as I can to stay with him.

"Sleep, Angel. All our problems will be solved in due time." He kisses me and sighs.

I close my eyes and settle next to him. He's right. I can't solve our problems without facing them and right now, I just want to share his bed and his warmth.

Part Twenty-Four

I set down the book I'm trying to read. Greyson has yet to return from the Home Office. There was a messenger waiting when we arrived back from the tailor's. I smile thinking of how the duke had apologized to me for having to leave. As if I am more important than the prime minister or the regent. That was five hours ago.

I pace to the bed and back. A restless urge has taken a hold of me. If I were a different person with friends, I'd go and spend time with them. But I have no friends and so am stuck in this house waiting for Greyson to return. A knock sounds.

"Come in," I call out, hoping it's a diversion.

Johnson comes in. "My lord, I'm sorry to disturb you, but there is a gentleman downstairs who wishes to speak to you."

"Me?" I'm surprised. "I don't know anyone who would want to talk to me unless it's my uncle."

"No, sir. It's not your uncle or your father. It's a gentleman who talks to his Grace once in a while, but he won't leave any message with me. He says he has to talk to you." Johnson shrugs.

I tug on my coat, making sure I look neat. If it is one of Greyson's friends, I don't want to make a bad impression. "Take me to him, Johnson."

"Yes, my lord."

I follow the valet downstairs to Greyson's study. I open the door and step in, instantly plunged into darkness. No lights had been lit in the room. I stay by the door, worried this is a trap, but no one rushes towards me.

"Are you in here?" I feel foolish, but I need to make sure the stranger hasn't left.

"Yes. I have a message for Greyson and I need you to deliver it." The voice comes from the area around the fireplace.

Even though I know where he is, I choose to stay by the door. "Why not leave it with the butler or Johnson?"

"It's a verbal message. We can't take a chance at writing it down." A whisper trails through the room as if he has shifted and his clothes rub together.

"Are you a spy?" Fascination rushes through me. I wonder if Greyson is a spy as well.

"I am what I need to be. Tell Greyson that our small friend is expanding. This friend is eyeing more than his fair share of the pie."

"Right. Small friend expanding. Eyeing more than his fair share of the pie." I nod to myself since he can't see me in the darkness. "Got it. Anything else?"

"I'll be back in a day or two with more information. Make sure the duke gets the message."

Before I can think, the stranger is standing in front of me. I still cannot see any features on his face. The darkness impedes my vision. A finger caresses my cheek and lips brush over mine. He's gone. I can't tell if he leaves by the door behind me or through the garden door. I press a finger to my lips and laugh.

I find my way to one of the chairs by the fireplace and sit down. Leaning my head back, I shut my eyes. I hate the dark because I never know what lurks in the shadows, but I also love it because it hides my flaws from others. This time it embraces me and I find myself sliding into sleep, wondering what it is about me that possess strangers to kiss me in the darkness.

"Angel, wake up."

I open my eyes to see Greyson kneeling beside the chair. His hand rests on my shoulder with a gentle touch. Smiling, I rub my fingertips over his frowning lips. I lean forward and kiss him. His lips mold to mine and we feast on each other. His hand moves from my shoulder to the base of my head and cups me. I angle my head to give him permission to take the kiss deeper. His tongue invades my mouth and strokes behind my upper teeth. I shiver in delight as my shaft stiffens. I push closer to him, gripping his shoulders for support.

He chuckles and pulls away. "I need to wake you up more often, love." He glances around the room. "Why were you sitting in the dark?"

Blinking, I try to remember anything other the taste of Greyson's lips. "Oh, Johnson told me there was a gentleman who wanted to talk to me. When I got down here, the room was totally dark. I stayed near the door in case I needed to get away."

The duke frowns. "What did the gentleman want?"

"He had a message for you that he didn't trust to anyone but me. Are you a spy?" I don't expect him to answer.

"I am what I need to be." He stands and moves towards the garden door that is ajar.

"That's the same thing he said to me when I asked him if he was a spy."

He relaxes. "What did he want you to tell me?" Moving back to me, he pulls me up from the chair and sits. I'm now curled up on his lap, which I'm discovering is my favorite place to be.

"He said to tell you your small friend is expanding and has his eye on more than his fair share of the pie." I press a soft kiss on his chin.

"Damn." Greyson growls. I can't tell if it's caused by my words or my actions.

I untie his cravat and get the first few buttons on his shirt undone before he stops my hands. I give him an innocent stare. He shakes his head and laughs. Lifting me to my feet, he stands. He keeps my hand in his and leads the way out of the room.

"Do you have to go somewhere?" I ask, trying to keep the disappointment out of my voice.

"Johnson, we'll have supper up in my room," Greyson informs the valet as we stroll by.

"It'll be ready in an hour or two, your Grace."

I glance back to see Johnson smiling after us. I can't keep

the grin off my face. I don't think the duke is planning on going anywhere for the rest of the night. Need hits me, making my prick hard. Reaching out, I cup one of Greyson's buttocks and squeeze.

He gets the door to his bedroom open and pushes me through. Before I can say anything, he kisses me.

Part Twenty-Five

I open to him and allow his tongue to thrust into my mouth. My hands twine into his hair and his arms wrap around my waist to pull me close to him. Rocking against each other, I rub my prick on his. The barrier of our clothes frustrates me.

Pulling away, I start to unbutton his shirt. I want to feel his skin. Soon Greyson's shirt finds its way to the floor and I'm running my hands over his chest. Rough hair curls around my fingers. I scrape my thumbnail over the hard nipple. Groaning, his grip tightens on my hips and pulls me even closer to him.

I'm not sure what to do. I stare up at him, trying to figure out what I can do to make him moan. My hand hesitates on his chest.

Looking at me, he must sense my confusion because he takes my hand and presses it hard to his chest. "Do you remember what I did to you last night and earlier today?"

I blush, but nod.

"Then do to me what made you feel good. You won't disgust me, love." He brushes his lips over mine.

I breathe deep, trying to settle my nerves. I know he won't laugh at me. I flex my fingers, kneading the muscles under them. He moans and shivers. Cupping my elbow, he leads me to the bed.

"I think we should both be sitting while you explore." He laughs and winks.

"Yes." My knees are feeling wobbly and I'm happy for the support of the mattress.

Leaning back against the headboard, he holds his arms out to me. I shake my head and kneel next to him. His hands drop to the blanket.

"I'm all yours. Do what you wish."

He is laid out before me like a vast frontier I long to explore.

My trembling hands trail down the crisp hair on his chest to where it thins to a single line that disappears under his trousers. Shooting a quick glance up at his face, I see his blazing blue eyes are half closed and he is watching me intently. My hand hovers over the bulge covered by fabric.

"Everything or nothing. It's up to you, Angel." He isn't going to force me.

I run my fingers lightly over the length of his shaft. He takes a sharp breath and a surge of power rushes through me. My hands tremble as I reach out and unbutton his trousers. He's silent, but raises his hips to help me strip his clothes off. Soon he is naked and I finally have a chance to look at him.

His body is muscled and trim. He doesn't seem to be sliding into dissipation like many noblemen. I skate my hand over the dark circle of flesh on his chest. It hardens, so I flick it with a fingernail. He jerks and I lean down to lick his nipple with my tongue. He tastes salty from sweat, but his own unique taste still dances in my mouth. His hands entwine in my hair and urge me to move to his other nipple. I give it my undivided attention. Soon it is red and Greyson is moaning.

As much as I am enjoying teasing him with my tongue, I find the brush of his hard shaft against my thigh is distracting me. Pulling back, I glance down at his groin and a groan escapes my throat. His cock isn't as long as mine, but it's thicker. The flared head has been revealed in all its red moist glory. I swipe my thumb over the wet tip and bring it to my lips. His seed tastes bitter and salty.

His intake of breath caused me to glance up and I see him staring at me with intense interest. A sudden attack of shyness hits me. I look back down at his shaft. Since I've never done anything like this before, I'm not sure what I should do. I know I want to give him as much pleasure as he gave me earlier today. I clasp my hand around him and stroke gently.

"I won't break, love." He wraps his hand around mine and shows me the rhythm he enjoys.

Soon I'm pumping my hand up and down his shaft with a rough and quick motion. His hips move with me, thrusting him into my palm. The seed leaking from the slit in his head helps to ease the way. My other hand never settles in one place. I play with his nipples, and then slide down to fondle and squeeze his sac. I feel his muscles start to tense.

"Angel, I'm close." His voice is hoarse and filled with passion.

I frown, not sure what he means.

"I'm going to spill my seed." How he manages to explain while breathing so hard is beyond me.

"Oh." I find I want to have him empty his seed into my mouth like I did to him earlier. "Wait."

A strangled chuckle comes from his chest. "I don't think you know what you're asking me."

"I want to take you in my mouth and give you the same pleasure you gave me." I wiggle around, stretching out on the bed beside him. My hand keeps stroking him, but I place my mouth round the tip of his shaft. I remember how he swallowed me down, so I open my mouth and suck him in. When the head hits the back of my throat, I gag and pull off him, coughing and embarrassed.

His hand runs over the top of my head. "You're new at this, love. Don't try to take it all in at once. In time, you'll be able to taste all of me, but for now, a little will be fine."

Nodding, I compose myself. I can do this. I want to do this. Greyson has given me more pleasure than I ever imagined possible. I'd like to return some of it to him. I place my lips around him again and take the tip of his shaft in.

I swirl my tongue around the silky hardness. I tease him with my teeth, not enough to cause pain. I can feel his blood pulsing through the vein on the underside of his shaft. I pull off with a pop and lick to the base. He groans and I have the feeling he's enjoying my inexperience.

I go back to the tip and take a little more in this time. I apply suction to it, massaging it the best I can with my tongue. He's panting now and moving his hips in short thrusts, trying hard not to push it all the way into my mouth, I suppose. Silently, I vow to learn how to take all of him in.

"Love, going to spill." He tugs on my hair.

I know he wants me to pull off and not swallow his seed, but I want to taste him. He did the same for me and I can do no less. I shake my head and increase the licking and suction.

"Oh God," he cries out as his hands cup my head and his seed fills my mouth in short bursts.

I try hard to swallow it all, but soon it is leaking from the sides of my mouth. When he is finally still, I pull off and rest my head on his hip.

"Angel, come here." His hands reach out and lift me up to lie on his chest.

Our faces are inches apart and he smiles at me. His eyes are hazy with exhaustion and love. He runs a finger over my chin, cleaning off his seed from my face. He brings our mouths together and moans. I love the salty bitterness flavor. Our tongues duel as he searches out every inch of my mouth and touches it.

His hands cup my buttocks and rub me against his hip. "Move, love. Take your pleasure now."

It wouldn't be long. I could feel my sac tighten and my cock beg for release while I dined on my lover. A few hard thrusts against his body and I'm spilling my seed as well. I cry out and press my face into his shoulder.

When my shudders fade, he climbs out of bed. Greyson undresses me and then cleans us both. By the time he comes back to bed, I'm almost asleep. He settles, his chest to my back, and wraps his arms around me. I grasp his hand in mine and lay them over my heartbeat.

"I love you, Angel," his voice whispers in my ear.

I love you too, I want to say, but sleep has captured me and I tumble without saying the words.

Part Twenty-Six

"Angel, will you join me tonight?" Greyson's tone is casual, but I can tell he's nervous about asking me to go with him.

A shiver of fear races through me. Where does he want me to go? He has gone to balls and other parties without me since I moved in with him. I've never wanted to go and he's never asked me. "Where?"

"I'm attending the Marquis of Beckenworth's ball tonight. He's an old friend from my school days. This is his wife's first society party. I promised I would come." He tugs on his cuffs and I smile at his nervousness.

Does he really want me to go with him? Is he afraid I'll say no?

"I'm not sure it's a good idea. My father could be there." I fear seeing Father again. I don't believe I'm strong enough to fight if he's there.

"You're going to have to face him at some time, love. You're free of him." Greyson kneels in front of me.

He's right but for so long my father ruled me and controlled every aspect of my life. I fear giving him a chance to capture me again. "I know but I'm afraid."

I'm not afraid to admit that. I know he'll support me no matter what my decision is.

"I know you are. You're strong enough to deal with him." He takes my hands in his and stares up at me. "I'll be there."

That statement plus the feeling that he wants me to go makes me decide to take a chance. I'll go out into the world where I never fit in. I'll face the people who laugh and gossip about me because of the golden god in front of me. Maybe it is time for me to start proving I can run my own life. "I'll go with you."

"Thank you." He presses a gentle kiss on the knuckles of

my hand and stands. "Would you like to pick out your clothes or should I?"

"You chose." I'm trying not to panic. I'm shaking at the thought of seeing Father again.

Thirty minutes later, I'm ready. The butler opens the front door and I see the carriage waiting for us at the bottom of the steps. I take a deep breath. For the first time since I ran from Society, I'm willingly returning all for the love of the man standing beside me. I'm making him happy. For now that's all that matters.

We settle in the carriage and the footman closes the door. Greyson sits next to me and takes my hand.

"I wanted you to come so you could meet Harry."

I squeeze his hand and stare out the window. I calm myself. Greyson is here. He won't leave me to face them alone. Even though he can't hold my hand, I know he'll be supporting me.

To take my mind off the ball, I ask, "Why do you want us to meet?"

"Harry's my oldest friend. Our estates border each other and we've grown up together. I want the man I consider my brother to meet the man I love."

A tingle fills my heart like always when he says he loves me. "The Marquis knows about you?" I find it hard to believe the Marquis tolerates Greyson's preferences.

"Yes, he does. He's known for a long time. He helped me deal with my marriage and made me let go of my guilt."

I run my thumb over his knuckle. I know Greyson still feels shame and sadness over the truth of his marriage.

"I'd be honored to meet your friend."

He brings my hand up to his mouth and kisses my palm. "Harry will like you. Maybe you can befriend and help Alice, Harry's wife. She's young and rather shy. I think you'll have much in common with her." He tugs off one of my gloves.

"Was theirs an arranged marriage?" I moan as he sucks one

of my fingers into his moist heat.

"No," he replies, resting our hands on his thigh. "It's a love match. Alice's father wasn't happy about it. Harry had a reputation as a rake. Her father figured Harry would break her heart, but Harry's madly in love with her so there's no worry about that."

The carriage stops outside a magnificent house. The windows are bright with light and people are making their way up the steps to the front door. Greyson hops out and I follow more slowly, tugging my glove back on.

He walks ahead of me and I must fight back the urge to touch him. We may do as we wish in private, but in public we must not show any more affection for each other than two friends would.

"Angel," he says in a low tone.

Looking up, I see he's made his way to the front of the receiving line. I hurry to join him.

"Harry, this is Angel." Greyson gestures to me.

The Marquis of Beckenworth is a dark-haired, roughly handsome man. He smiles and shakes my hand. "The mysterious Angel we've been hearing about. We'll have to talk later." The Marquis turns to his wife. "Alice, this is Greyson's Angel."

As I take her hand and bow, she says, "I believe we've already met."

I look up into kind green eyes and I realize who told Greyson my name. "It's a pleasure to meet you again, my lady."

"I'll save a dance for you." She smiles as we move farther into the ballroom.

I don't feel as nervous now. I have a friend of my own aside from Greyson. I glance at the duke as we start to mingle in the crowd.

"Now I know who told you my name."

"I'd watched you for a few nights. I figured Alice would be the best choice to approach you. You didn't seem as nervous around women." He winks at me.

"It wasn't nerves. It was fear." I search the crowd to see if I can spot my father.

"Angel, I see someone I have to talk to. Would you excuse me?" Greyson nods towards the other side of the room.

I look around quick and spot an alcove I can hide in. "Go ahead. I'll hide out here." I gesture to the wall.

"Good. I'll find you later." He strolls off into the crush.

I stomp down on the twinge of fear. I can deal with being by myself for a while. I don't need him spending all his time with me. There is no way my father would make a scene here if he should arrive.

I watch as the dancing starts. Harry leads Alice out on the floor and I marvel at the love shining in their eyes. It's obvious that they care for each other deeply. I edge out of my hiding place and start to move around the edge of the dance floor. I nod to people whose gaze I meet, but I don't stop to talk to anyone. The music ends after the first dance, but the conversations continue.

"Robert, there you are. I've been looking for you. Will you be my partner for this next dance?" Alice places her hand on my arm and smiles up at me.

There is no way I can say no. Nodding, I escort her out on the floor. Our steps are perfectly matched as we waltz. At first, she is content just to dance. After a minute, she looks at me.

"Are you happy?"

Part Twenty-Seven

Am I happy? It's a strange question and I don't think anyone ever cared to know if I was happy. Yet looking into Alice's eyes, I can see that she is really interested in my answer.

I glance around the room, trying to see if I can find Greyson. He is leaving the room. Worry shoots through me, but I crush it. There is nothing that can happen to me here. People who are more Greyson's friends than my father's surround me. Also, I must learn how to deal with being by myself. The duke can't live his life attached to me. I've proven I can be strong if I need to be.

"Robert?" Alice's soft inquiry brings my attention back to her.

"I think I am. It's hard to say. I've only been away from my father for a week or so. Can a life change that quickly? Is happiness that easy an emotion to gain?" I frown.

She stares at me for a moment and I wonder if maybe I should have just said yes. Then she nods.

"I know what you mean." Her gesture includes all the people dancing around us. "I'm not sure I'm made to be a society queen. I don't really fit in here."

I laugh. "My dear lady, if you don't fit in, then I have no chance to ever be a part of this strange world."

Her laugh trickles from her lips and those around us turn to stare. Some of them smile and nod. Others frown as if there shouldn't be any joy here. I shrug.

"Are you happy, my lady?" I twirl her around until we are close to the edge of the dancers, so when the music stops, I bow and offer her my arm.

Taking it, she tilts her head and stares off for a moment. I don't say anything, just lead her toward a footman. The young man holds a tray of refreshments. I hand her one and she nods.

"Yes, I am. My father believed Harry would break my heart. I couldn't convince him that Harry would rather die than hurt me." Alice's eyes gleam with love.

I understand what she's saying. I think Greyson feels the same way. We continue to chat and mingle with her guests. Tension slowly disappears from my shoulders. My eyes no longer scan the crowd, searching for either my father or Greyson.

"How dare you?" A voice cuts through our conversation.

Alice and I turn to find my father standing behind us. Fear causes me to freeze. His eyes burn me and I feel the scars on my back tighten. I've faced his anger before and have paid for it with my blood. Alice's fingers grip my arm and I'm brought back to the ballroom where my father is shouting at me.

"You dare to show your face at this young lady's ball. You're nothing but an embarrassment. Where is your lover, son?"

Before he can say the words, Alice steps in front of me. "Watch what you say, Lord Williamson. Robert is my friend. You are not." She glances around and gestures to a footman. "Find my husband and bring him to me."

Growling, Father reaches for her. I push my fear away. He mustn't touch her. I know the pain his hands can inflict. I block his hand and insert myself between them. "Not here, Father. Please, not now."

I'm not sure why I'm begging now when it has never worked before, but I don't want Alice to be hurt or upset over the scene my father seems determined to create. He spits at me.

"Do you know what he is?" He swings his hand towards me.

I don't move. Let him inflict the pain on me. I'm used to it. I refuse to allow him anywhere near Alice. The crack of his flesh meeting mine rings through the air. My head wants to whip back from the force of it, but I control it. I'll not give him the satisfaction of seeing me wince.

"He is a friend, Williamson. I think you had better leave." The Marquis of Beckenworth makes his way through the throng, followed by two large footmen.

A hand touches my back and I breathe in the familiar scent of my lover. He's returned just when I need him the most.

Greyson doesn't say anything. It is the Marquis who takes charge and orders the footmen to escort my father out. Father doesn't fight them. He gives me a hate-filled stare.

"Some day you won't be surrounded by these fake friends of yours. I'll get you back," he hisses before he turns around to leave.

The Marquis gestures and the musicians start playing. The guests pretend not to notice the four of us slipping away. When we get to an empty room, Greyson turns me to look at my cheek. I'm sure there's a red handprint marring my skin, but it doesn't bother me. I stare over his shoulder at Alice.

"I'm sorry to ruin your ball, my lady," I apologize to her.

She laughs and shakes her head. "You didn't ruin it, Angel. In fact, I'm sure it'll be the most talked about ball of the Season. Besides, they all came here expecting something scandalous to happen anyway." She moves up to stand beside Greyson. "Are you all right?"

I nod. "He's done worse to me." I pull away from Greyson's touch. "I think I'll go home now." I'm tired and my face hurts. I just want to crawl into bed, hide under the covers and try not to think about my father.

"Of course. I'll go order the carriage." Greyson brushes a kiss over my mouth. He shakes Harry's hand and hugs Alice.

There is a moment of silence after he leaves, then I ask Harry a question. "Why are you still his friend?"

The surprise on his face tells me he's never considered turning his back on Greyson. "He's been my best friend for years. He doesn't flaunt his preferences, but even if he did, I'd stand by him." Harry gives me a hard look. "Don't hurt him, Angel. You've become his world and you have more power to destroy him than any other person."

I nod, letting him know I heard the threat and I'll remember.

I take Alice's hand to kiss it. She wraps her arms around me and gives me a hug. After hesitating, I hug her back. She kisses my cheek.

"Don't be a stranger," she whispers in my ear.

"I won't. You should return to your guests. The carriage should be out front by now."

We separate at the door. They head back to the ballroom. I exit the house to find Greyson standing by the carriage. He gestures for me to join him. I stare at him for a moment. In the flickering light of the street lamps, I see concern mixing with love in his eyes. I'm beginning to see what Harry meant. I have the power to hurt Greyson far more than he could ever hurt me. That thought makes me shiver and I run down the steps to him, knowing I would never chance breaking this man's heart.

Greyson isn't looking at me when I get to his side. He's staring across the street. Following his gaze, I see a man standing in the shadows. I know he's the one the duke is looking at. The man nods once. Glancing up at Greyson, I see him give the man a slight smile.

I'm intrigued, but a throb of pain reminds me I want to go home. I climb into the carriage and Greyson sits next to me. He wraps his arms around me and lets me lean my head on his shoulder. His hand strokes my hair. I sigh and relax. The encounter could have been worse, but I didn't collapse into a pathetic coward.

"You did it, Angel. You stood up to him." Greyson's voice rumbles in his chest and I feel safe.

"I just didn't want him to hurt Alice." I'm not sure there's a lot of courage in that.

"Harry will thank you for that. Of course, if your father had put his hands on Alice, Harry probably would have called him out." Greyson chuckled. "Which would have been disastrous for your father."

I'm not ready to laugh yet. A little swell of pride rolls through me. In a small way, I did stand up to my father. Hope begins to unfurl like a flower and I feel as if my freedom is within my reach. All I have to do is grab it, knowing that Greyson will catch me if I fall.

We pull up outside his house. I kiss him quick and then climb out of the carriage. After handing my coat, hat and gloves to the butler, I make my way up stairs to our bedroom.

Greyson starts to follow me when the butler stops him and tells him something under his breath. I glance behind me and Greyson stares up at me. I can tell he is torn between coming with me and taking care of what the butler wishes of him. I smile and nod, letting him know I'll be all right. He smiles back and blows me a kiss.

Johnson is waiting in our room when I get there. "Is His Grace coming up as well?"

"Not at the moment, Johnson. He has some business to attend to." I unbutton my coat. I've gotten used to having the valet in the room with me while I dress and undress, but I still don't allow him to help me.

He huffs. "They never leave him alone. They are constantly badgering him for advice or help." The rotund man putters around the room, picking up my clothes as I discard them.

I nod. I don't have the energy to engage him in conversation at the moment. Climbing into bed, I bury my aching face into a pillow.

"Goodnight, my lord," Johnson murmurs as he leaves the room.

I don't acknowledge him. Sleep is gaining ground and I don't want to fight it. I just hope no nightmares haunt my dreams.

Part Twenty-Eight

I feel the mattress dip as Greyson slides under the covers and joins me in our bed. He wraps an arm around my waist to pull me tight against him, my back to his chest. His lips brush over the bruise on my cheek. I sigh and the dull throbbing of my face fades.

"Does your face still hurt, love?" His breath bathes my ear.

"A little. I'm better now that you're here." I press closer to his warmth.

"I'm sorry. I wanted to come upstairs with you as soon as we got home, but it was important I deal with the person waiting for me." He moves my hair out of the way and whispers a kiss over the nape of my neck.

I hear the guilt in his voice and that isn't what I want. I said those words because they were true, not because I wanted to manipulate him. "I know." I roll over so we are face-to-face. "Is something wrong?"

A frown mars his forehead, but he shakes his head. "Nothing for you to worry about, love."

Why do I have the feeling that he's patting me on the head like he would an overly curious child? I bite my lip to keep from complaining. "I know you're involved with the government, Greyson. I've heard numerous times that you have the ear of the regent and of the prime minister. I get the feeling you do more than just give advice when they ask." I put my finger over his mouth when he starts to speak. "You've brought me into your home. You've given me more freedom and love then I've ever known. You also tell me your heart belongs to me, but I know nothing about you. Why are there strangers coming and going at all hours of the day and night? Why when the Home Office requests your presence, do you drop everything and go? Who was that stranger the other night and what did that message I delivered for him mean?"

As the duke stares at me, I can tell he's thinking, trying to decide how much to tell me or if he will tell me anything. I pull away from him and climb out of bed. A chill shivers down my spine. I wonder what has come over me to make me confront Greyson like this, but I won't back down.

I stop in front of the fireplace. Turning, I look back through the darkness to where I know he still lies on the bed. "I'm not fragile. You told me that yourself. You say you love me, but as what? Do you love me as a man? Am I someone you can tell all your secrets to or am I merely a plaything for you to pull out when you get bored?"

Tears well up in my eyes. I try to swallow around the lump in my throat. I know how I want him to answer. I want— No, I need him to see me as his equal because if he doesn't then in reality I am no better off than I was when I lived with my father.

I hear the bedclothes rustle and then I see him kneeling in the middle of the mattress, holding his hand out to me.

"Angel, my love, come back to bed. Please join me and I'll tell you what I can."

I want to be strong and demand he tell me everything right now. But the room is cold and I can hear love in his voice. I don't want to hurt him. It is just something is inside me, demanding to be seen as a real person, not a child or a helpless creature.

"Please."

Returning to the bed, I take his hand and let him pull me back under the covers. Greyson settles me into his arms. I rest my head on his chest and smile as his hand strokes over my back.

He takes a deep breath. "Before I got married, I was a hellion. I'd rather cause trouble than be respectable. I indulged myself with gambling, dueling and women."

I stiffen and he chuckles.

"I might have been a hellion, love, but I wasn't stupid. I knew I had to keep my true preferences discrete and hidden from the Ton. Even now there are very few of my friends who know where my interests truly lie." His hand stops its caress and I can tell he's remembering the past. "I was bored. There was something missing from the life I was leading, but I never understood what. Then my father told me I had to marry. So like any dutiful son, I did. Maria was beautiful and from a good family. If she was intelligent, kind or loving, I have no idea. I ignored her after our wedding day except for when I bedded her."

Tension slowly tights his muscles. I know thinking of his wife hurts him. I rub my hand over his stomach, trying to ease the pain with my touch. He relaxes a little.

"I got her with child quickly. As soon as I could after my first son was born, I planted my seed in her womb again. For once luck smiled on me and she gave me another son. Now I had the heir I needed to carry on the family line and another son in case something happened to the first. I was relieved because that meant I didn't have to have anything to do with Maria anymore. I could allow her to do as she pleased as long as it didn't interfere with my life."

This time it is Greyson who climbs out of bed and paces around the room. I pile pillows behind me and lean against them while I watch him move.

"I listen to myself and think what a horrid selfish man I was back then. I didn't care how it made Maria feel. I didn't care if I was breaking her heart or not. As long as it didn't disrupt my life, I was indifferent to her. I abandoned her in the country and made my way back to town as soon as I could." He scrubs a hand over his face. "I know now that I broke her heart. She loved me, even though I had been indifferent to her from our first meeting. I never did anything intentionally cruel. In my eyes, leaving her in the country wasn't cruel. I was a selfish arrogant bastard. I realized my guilt only after she died."

I'm not sure what to say. I don't know how to fix it. I know how being ignored by someone who should love you creates the deepest wounds. A sob ripples the silence. I watch in horror as Greyson collapses to his knees and cries. Scrambling out of bed, I race to him. I drop to the floor next to him and for the first time in our relationship, I offer my shoulder for him to cry on. For this moment in time, I am the strong one who will help heal a small part of his wounded soul.

"I've been a terrible father, Angel. I've ignored my sons because I resented the marriage that produced them. They're kept in the country, or sent away to school, so I didn't have to look at them."

"You only did what your father did with you. Yet you recognize what is wrong. Maybe you can still fix your relationship with them. Bring them to town, or better yet, go to the country and spend time with them," I suggest, not sure if I'm the right person to offer advice.

"Would you go with me? Would you help me learn who my children are?" Greyson meets my gaze with hope.

"Yes."

I brush my lips over his. His unique taste mixes with his tears and they dance upon my tongue. I stroke along his teeth, learning the ridges. He shivers as the tip of my tongue teases the sensitive area behind his front teeth. I bite his bottom lip and then soothe it with a lick. I suck on it and let it go with a pop.

He wraps his arms around me and pulls me tight to him. Our mouths crush together. Our tongues duel. His hands grasp my ass. Mine bury in his hair. Each new kiss he gives me tastes more of passion than of sorrow.

Soon I straddle him as he sits on the floor, my legs gripping his hips. Our pricks rub together and I moan. His hands support me as I rock against him. I love the feel of his hard cock on me. He leans back, letting me lie on top of him while we move together.

"Angel, would you like to make love to me?"

I stop, staring at him in shock. He wants me to be inside him. I think about the sensations. How full I was with his prick in me. How my passion built at the base of my spine and then exploded. I remember lying beneath him and him loving me.

I look at him and shake my head. "I can't. I'm sorry." I stop moving and start to climb off him.

"No. Don't apologize. It's too soon. You need more time." He rolls and I'm on my back. He kisses me. "Is this all right?"

"Yes." I kiss him back, embracing him with my arms and legs. "Please."

He pulls away from me and goes to the table next to his bed. He reaches out, grabs a small jar and brings it back with him. He presses his hand to my thigh, asking me silently to move my legs farther apart. I hook my hands around my knees and pull them wide, offering all that I am to him.

"So beautiful," he whispers as his slick fingers caress my shaft and then slide down to fondle my sac.

I moan as he squeezes me once and then skims a fingertip over the soft skin behind them. Greyson teases my opening with a light tap while his other hand grasps my prick in a firm grip and strokes. My hips arch off the floor and I feel the pressure as he pushes his finger inside me. He coordinates his hand and finger. Soon I'm surrounded by the sensations of my shaft sliding through his hand and his fingers moving in me.

He slides three fingers in me, twisting as he reaches that special spot. His knuckles brush it and it feels as if lightning shoots through me.

"Oh," I gasp. "Greyson, I need you inside me. Now."

The loss of the duke's fingers makes an empty space inside of me, but the pressure of his cock pushing in soon replaces it. I take a deep breath and relax, allowing him to ease all the way into me. He rests his hands on either side of my head and leans down to kiss me.

"May I move now, love?" His voice is hoarse and strained. I can tell not moving is a struggle for him.

"Yes, take me." I tilt my hips, encouraging him to move.

He moves and this time it's a bit rougher and harder, but that is how I want it. I feel him deep inside my passage. My balls tighten and I know my climax is building. I wrap my arms around his shoulders, holding on as my passion explodes from me. My seed coats our stomachs as he continues to thrust. He moves faster and harder, his breath coming in pants. My passage massages his shaft, milking his pleasure from him.

"Angel," Greyson cries out as wet heat spills into me. His forehead comes to rest on my shoulder as his hips slowly stop moving.

We rest on the floor for several minutes, both trying to regain enough strength to move to the bed. I smooth my hand up and down the duke's back, just enjoying the feel of his skin under my fingertips. He rolls to the side with a sigh.

He brushes a kiss over my lips. "Thank you."

I smile and kiss him back. He climbs to his feet and walks to the dresser. I lie on the floor, watching him clean himself. Something is different about the duke. Maybe there is less sorrow in his eyes or less tension in his shoulders. I guess I didn't realize how much guilt he still felt because of how he treated his wife. I hope talking to me about her helps heal some of the wounds he carries.

He comes back to me and cleans my body. I let him, even though I am capable of doing it. I know he needs to take care of me. When he finishes, he helps me up and we make our way to the bed.

We cuddle beneath the blankets. I rest my head on his chest and wrap an arm around his waist. As I fall asleep, I hear him whisper, "I'm sorry, Maria." A smile crosses my lips. He'll be all right now.

Part Twenty-Nine

I am surrounded by warmth as I slowly wake up the next morning. Greyson is curled behind me. His prick is hard and nestles in the crease of my ass. His hand curls around my hip. Murmuring something I can't make out, he begins rocking us together.

"Oh," I gasp as his teeth nip at the sensitive spot behind my ear. I push back against him and a shiver runs over my skin as the head of his cock bumps my opening.

He rubs his body on mine, reaching for the small jar sitting on the nightstand. I adore the feel of his chest pressed to me. When he settles back behind me, his hand slides under my thigh and lifts my leg forward, allowing better access.

Slick fingers tease me. I rock my hips and bite my lip. I don't want to beg him to take me, but my body knows what it wants. "Please" slips out, making him smile against my neck. My skin flushes and somehow he knows it's because I'm embarrassed, not because I'm aroused.

"Never be embarrassed to ask for what you want, Angel. I like knowing you crave my touch." His warm breath plays over my neck, distracting me as the tip of his finger slides inside me. I still ache from last night, but it doesn't matter. All I can think about is having him inside me again.

No matter how many times we do this, I will never get used to the feeling of fullness, and that's just from his fingers. He nibbles along my shoulder and pushes against my back. I roll on to my hands and knees, shamelessly offering myself to him. One finger becomes two and then three. Soon I'm rocking back on, begging without words for his touch.

"God," I moan as he touches a spot inside me that makes sparks dance in my eyes. "Again."

Greyson laughs. "Now you're demanding. Who knew such a

little wanton hid under that shy exterior?" He pushes his fingers farther in and twists them.

"Please." My voice breaks as he begins to rub over that spot with each thrust of his fingers.

Pleasure builds through my body. I can feel it shoot from my head down over my chest to pool at the base of my spine. My prick stiffens and my need grows. Lust ripples my skin as he wraps his rough hand around me and strokes.

"Greyson, I'm going to…" I lean my forehead down on the pillow in front of me. My breath disappears as my desire grabs hold of me and drains me of my seed.

I shudder and spill my essence, but Greyson doesn't let me go. He rolls me on to my back. Kneeling between my legs, he covers his own prick with the oil and settles the flared head against my opening.

"May I," he asks while slowly pushing into me.

I nod and relax, letting my lover into me, eager to feel him deep inside me. No hesitation or doubt. He fills me with one long thrust. Our moans float through the room. He waits for a moment, not willing to move until I tell him it's okay. With a small tilt of my hips, I encourage him to make love to me.

"So tight, love." His voice is harsh and his hands grip my hips tight.

I can't catch my breath as he rocks us together. The crown of his shaft hits the magic spot and I cry out. Pleasure begins to build in me and I can't keep still. My hips rise to meet each of his strokes.

"Move, love. Show me how much you love me." He takes my hand in his and wraps it around my shaft. "Please yourself."

My skin heats, but I can't tell if it's from embarrassment or desire. I've never touched myself. Fear of my father kept me from enjoying any of my life. "What do I do?"

He keeps his hand on mine and moves it down on my shaft. "Do to yourself what I did to make you spill your seed. Move as fast or as slow as you wish."

My first attempts are feeble. I'm not sure I can pleasure myself in front of him. Soon though, I find I have no choice. With each thrust of his prick into me, my own shaft slides through my hand. All I have to do is adjust the pressure.

"More," I plead, not sure how much more he can give me, but knowing I need something else.

"Certainly." He lifts my legs over his forearms and spreads me wider. This opens me even more and he pushes deeper inside.

I lose what rhythm I have and lose myself in the sensations he creates in me. He is becoming a part of me. It's as if with each thrust, he reaches deep into my soul until we'll never be separate people again.

"Greyson." I don't know what I'm saying or asking for. All I know is he is the only thing in my mind as my pleasure spills from me once again. My inner muscles tighten around him and my hips rock, milking his own climax from him.

"Love you," he cries, filling me deep inside with liquid heat. He's branding me and I welcome the warmth.

I wrap my arms around his shoulders when his arms start to tremble. I ease him down on top of me. I don't mind his weight pressing me into the mattress. In a primordial way, it makes me feel safe to have him surround me with his body. We rest with our breath mingling until our heartbeats stop racing.

He gives me another gentle kiss and then climbs from the bed. He grabs a cloth, wetting it to clean his body. After he's done, he brings another cloth for me. Greyson makes me lie still while he takes care of me.

He joins me in bed, wrapping his arms around me and pulling me tight to him. We fall asleep, our hearts beating as one.

Part Thirty

Greyson moves, waking me up as a knock sounds on the door. I open my eyes to see the duke climb out of bed.

"Will you be down for breakfast, your grace?" Johnson stands in the doorway.

"Bring a tray up for us," Greyson orders the valet while moving to the dresser.

"Yes, sir." Johnson leaves.

I admire my lover's form. Tall and muscular, he isn't a man who has let the late nights and rich drink of the Ton ruin his health. My prick tells me how much it agrees with my mind. Greyson turns and smiles at me.

He holds my robe out for me to slip on. "The rest of our discussion was postponed last night. I'm sorry."

I cup his cheek, turning his gaze to mine. "Don't apologize. Do you feel better now?"

He nods. "Yes, I do. I guess I still had some mourning left to do. I never realized how guilty I still felt about Maria. Thank you, love."

Our lips meet in a benediction. Promises are made as we kiss. I put my hand on his chest to feel his heart beating. Another knock sounds and we move apart. Greyson puts on a robe while I stand out of the way for the servants delivering the breakfast trays.

"Johnson." Greyson stops the valet before the man could leave.

"Yes, your grace?"

"Make sure we're not disturbed. Not by anyone for any reason."

"Yes, sir." Johnson bows and shuts the door behind him.

"We'll be able to talk without interruption now." He gestures towards the table.

We sit, quietly taking the edge off our hunger. My body aches from our loving earlier that morning, but I'm beginning to welcome those feelings. After a while, Greyson fills his cup with coffee and leans back in his chair.

"Shortly after I abandoned my wife in the country, I returned to Town. I fell into some of my old habits, but lucky for me, some powerful men were keeping an eye on me."

I stay silent. It is his story to tell and I can't rush him. He stands, making his way over to the window.

"One night I was approached by someone in the Home Office. They needed some information on a certain nobleman. Unfortunately none of their usual employees ran in his circles. It seemed we shared the same interests. The man asked me to befriend this lord and gather what information I could."

Unease tries to settle in my stomach. Will Greyson tell me he turned in a man like us? I'm not sure how I feel about that.

"I was reluctant at first. I didn't feel right about spying on a fellow member of our club." He gives me a small smile and a wink. "The prime minister's man assured me they knew all about his perversions. They didn't care about them."

He laughs. "Perversions such as ours are not talked about in polite society. Yet people tend to know about them and ignore what happens behind closed doors."

"Why were they interested in this particular man if not for blackmail?"

"Rumors had surfaced about a slave trafficking ring. White slavery. White girls were disappearing and sold to foreigners as slaves. Usually for sexual uses."

Something in Greyson's voice makes me think this type of slavery is the thing of nightmares.

"And this man had something to do with it," I ask, not wanting to dwell on the actual slavery.

"Yes but the Home Office wasn't sure how he was involved. They wanted me to find out. So I did. At first I did it to get rid of my boredom. Then when I began to see what these slavers did to these girls, I became angry and determined to shut them down."

Coming back to the table, he sets his cup down and takes my hand. I stand in response to his tug, allowing him to lead me to the couch opposite the bed. He sits and pulls me onto his lap.

"We shut that ring down and thus began my service to the Crown. I travel in circles most of their spies can't obtain, so I hear things they don't."

I rest my head on his shoulder. "Are you always so busy?"

"Normally no, but events are starting that could change the world and England must be ready for them. Each day, more information comes to light and it worries me." He sighs.

I wrap my arms around his waist and press close to him. "You have so many obligations, why would you choose to open your life to me?" I'm not looking for him to flatter me. I'm just trying to understand why.

He pushes me away so he can look down at my face. "It's no hardship to love you, Angel. You're the brightest spot in my life. Now that I've met you, held you and loved you, the rest of the world dims in comparison and I'm not concerned about it. You are the most important thing to me and I'd do anything to make you happy."

Tears glisten in his eyes and my gaze blurs with my tears as well.

"I believe you," I whisper against his lips. "Thank you."

"For what?" He presses kisses across my cheeks and eyes.

"For loving me. For trusting me."

"I have no other choice but to love you. For you've stolen my heart, Angel."

The kisses we share are slow and gentle. Just as the passion is about to burn out of control, Johnson's voice sounds from the other side of the door.

"Your grace."

"I thought I said we didn't want to be disturbed." Greyson rests his forehead on mine.

"I'm sorry, sir, but the same gentleman who showed up here the other night is back. He says it's important." Johnson sounds apologetic.

"Damn." Greyson smiles at me. "England calls, love. I'd prefer to stay up here with you all day, but the outside world says no."

I chuckle and climb off his lap. "I don't mind. I'll go for a ride. Maybe visit Uncle. If you're free when I return, we'll find something to occupy us for the afternoon."

The sudden flare of heat in Greyson's eyes tells me he's already thought of an activity. I find myself resenting the secret life my lover leads.

I give him a hard kiss. "Just to give you something to think about while you're doing your business."

He groans. "Cruel tease. Now get dressed and go for a ride before I forget about everything and take you back to bed." He taps my buttocks as he calls for Johnson. "Get in here and help me."

I find my riding clothes as Johnson and the duke joke with each other. I'm dressed before Greyson is ready, so I peck his cheek with a kiss and head downstairs. I order my gelding. While I'm pulling on my gloves and coat, I hear a sound. I turn and glance down the hallway towards Greyson's study.

A dark haired man stands in the doorway of the study, staring at me. Bright green eyes study me and I feel uncomfortable. The butler hands me my hat. The stranger nods, closing the door behind him.

I stumble once going down the steps when I remember that is the man who kissed me the other night. I wonder why he would do that. I shake my head, telling myself that it's really no concern. He didn't mean anything by it. Just a passing joke, I'm sure.

Part Thirty-One

I curl up in the window seat, staring out at a world I no longer fear being a part of. I've come to cherish my time here with Greyson. He has taught me strength and confidence. He's shown me that not all the people in the world are out to hurt me.

Noises come from the duke's study. The butler told me he's still meeting with the man from earlier this morning. I don't complain. There's nothing pressing for us to do, though I find myself thinking about our bed upstairs. The door to the drawing room opens.

"Here you are," Greyson says as he walks in.

I turn to face him with a smile on my face. It's been two hours since I kissed him and left for my ride. I have missed him. A glass shatters on the floor. The stranger standing behind Greyson stares at me as if he's seen a ghost. I'm puzzled since the man had seen me that morning. He stalks across the room and kneels in front of me.

I don't flinch as he reaches out to touch my face. I've learned that not every outstretched hand is going to do violence to me. I frown at Greyson though.

"Who are you?" The stranger's voice holds fear and disbelief.

"I'm—" I start to tell him.

"He's Lord Williamson's eldest son. He's Angel." Greyson comes to stand by me. He rests a hand on my shoulder and squeezes.

"This is your angel. Ah, that would explain it then." The man pulls his hand away, but remains at my feet. "I got only a glimpse of you and your hat shaded your face. I couldn't see the resemblance."

I stare down into the most unusual green eyes. They are as pale as the duke's prized jade elephant. They shine up at me and a flicker of a memory comes to me.

"I know you." This time I'm the one to reach out and touch a cheek.

"How is that possible?" The duke seems uneasy about this revelation.

"I'm surprised you do. You were so young." A sad smile graces the man's lips.

"Shade, answer me. How do you know Angel?" Greyson grabs Shade's arm, forcing him to his feet.

They move to the other side of the room where two chairs are set facing a fireplace. I follow, intrigued by this visit from my past. Shade stands, staring at the picture above the mantel. The expression on his face tells us he's become lost in memories. The duke sits in one of the chairs and I sink to the floor at his feet. It's my favorite spot unless I'm sitting on his lap.

"Shade, explain," Greyson demands.

Shade doesn't respond and I wonder if his memories choke him like mine do to me. Memories of a summer long ago race through my mind and I remember things I'd forgotten in my fight to survive my father's rage.

"It was during the summer of my tenth year. I was staying with my uncle and his family. I remember a groom with the most unusual green eyes. He was nice to me. Didn't treat me like a nuisance. I went about my days in complete ignorance. Then one morning, my tutor came to wake me up. We left my uncle's house within an hour. I never really knew why. I remember my aunt was crying. My uncle and my cousin were fighting and yelling." I recount those memories without thought.

"Your cousin? I thought your uncle only had one child." Greyson frowns.

"He does now. I had an older cousin. I walked out of my uncle's house and at the foot of the steps stood the green-eyed groom. His fists were clenched. Even as a child, I knew he was furious about something, but I sensed fear in him as well. I went home and a week later, my father informed me that my cousin was dead." There hadn't been any sadness in me. I didn't know him very well, but it was after his death that my father began my abuse. I was isolated as a child, kept from anyone who might influence me in any way.

"His name was Jonathon and we were lovers. I still remember his laugh. I can still smell him and at times, it's as if he's in the room with me." Shade turns to study me. "You look exactly like him. The night before you left, someone saw us together and told Jonathon's father. He was furious. Threatening to kill us both for dishonoring the family name."

I am startled. No one ever said I looked like Jonathon. All I remember of my cousin was a handsome, laughing young man with sparkling brown eyes. He never seemed bothered by me. I had noticed he liked the stables and the horses more than any other place. I guess now I understand why. Standing, I move to Shade. His pain is visible in his eyes. I can't imagine what it would be like to hurt that way. I reach out a cautious hand. He can accept it or reject it. He takes it in his and holds tight.

"I was thrown off the estate and threatened with death if I ever tried to see Jonathon again. I did try. I couldn't leave him to suffer alone. I tried for a week until someone told me he was dead." He bites his lips to keep from sobbing, though a single tear rolls down his cheek.

"How did he die?"

I glare at the duke. How could he ask that question when Shade is so upset? Greyson shrugs.

"He killed himself. Slit his wrists and lost too much blood before anyone found him." Shade slumps forward, as if saying that takes all his strength.

I feel the scars at my wrists burn. My uncle had been unable to save his own son, but by saving his nephew, he had kept alive another embarrassment to the family name. Why would he choose to do that when he caused his own son to take his life? Looking at Shade with a closer gaze, I realize my uncle also broke this man's soul.

"I must leave." Shade yanks his hand from mine. "This is too much."

He nods to Greyson and leaves. Going back to the duke, I curl up on his lap. The safety I always feel engulfs me when his arms wrap around me and pulls me close to him. Shade's memories shake me to my core. I have forgotten much in my fight to survive within the walls of my prison.

"That explains a lot," he mutters against my ear.

It explains a lot, but there is still much I want to know. Tomorrow I'll search out my uncle and find out the truth. Is my cousin the reason he is supporting me? Does he truly accept what I am or is it merely penance for the life my cousin took? I wonder if the mistakes of the past will build a solid enough foundation for my future?

My mind is occupied with the information I've received. I don't notice that Greyson moves me so that I'm straddling him. It's his fingers on the closure of my trousers that brings my attention back to us. I look down to see him undoing the buttons and pushing the fabric out of the way. Without any help from me, he manages to free my shaft. I gasp as he grips it tight and pumps once with his hand.

"I think it's been too long since I've touched you, love." His blue eyes dance with laughter.

"I believe my body agrees with you." I moan, lifting my hips a little to give him better access to my prick.

He varies his strokes. Some are hard and fast. Some are slow and gentle. His thumb brushes my foreskin back, playing with the head of my cock. He teases the slit and pushes inside the opening just enough to make me hiss from the bite of pain.

His other hand supports my ass while urging me to move. Soon I'm thrusting into the warm rough tunnel his fingers create for me. He leans forward, his lips fastening on the sensitive vein throbbing in my neck. As his teeth nibble along my skin, he sweeps his palm over the exposed head of my prick, gathering the seed leaking out, and he uses it to ease my thrusts.

"Greyson," I groan, my balls tightening and desire pooling at the base of my spine.

"It's all right, love. I want to smell you and taste you. Show me your pleasure."

His whispers inflame me. I brace my hands on the back of the chair and thrust faster. Lights spark in my eyes and my back arches as my seed spills from me into his hand and onto his stomach. He keeps stroking, milking me dry until finally I slump against him, my head on his shoulder.

"Sit up for a moment." He supports me as I push myself back up so we're face-to-face again. He holds up his hand covered with my seed. My prick stirs and my blood heats as I watch him lick his hand clean. "Come taste yourself." He offers me his mouth.

I crush our lips together, sweeping my tongue through his mouth. I taste the salty bitterness of my seed and I moan. I devour his mouth, biting his bottom lip and soothing it with my tongue. I stroke the roof of his mouth and shivers rack his body. I want our tastes to mingle.

I push off him and fall to my knees in front of him. I fumble with the buttons on his trousers. He chuckles and helps me. Soon his fat prick is free and it seems to be begging for my mouth. I encircle the base of his cock with my thumb and forefinger, creating a tight ring around it.

Leaning closer, I flatten my tongue and lick up the vein that runs up the underside of the shaft. A deep groan catches my attention and I glance up to see Greyson watching me with intense focus. I can't help the smile that comes to my face. I know I have total control of the duke at that moment. He grins back, somehow knowing what I'm thinking.

I suck just the head of his cock into my mouth. I work the tip of my tongue into his slit, tasting his seed, and the need to have him flood my mouth with it surges in me. I pull away from him and stroke my hand up and down in a quick pumping motion. He groans, this time resting his head back on the chair. His hands tangle in my hair and I feel a slight pressure from them. He wants my mouth.

I'm a little more experienced now, so I take more of his length in and bath it with my tongue. His hands help me learn the angle and pace he enjoys the most. My one hand continues stroking him each time I bob my head. My other hand searches out the spheres hanging beneath his prick. I roll them together and fondle them. They draw up tight and I know he is getting close to spilling.

I suck harder, demanding my love's seed. He begins to thrust, trying not to overwhelm me with his entire length. I moan and the vibration of my noise causes him to shudder. I hum again and he cries out.

"Angel," he pleads with me as if he's waiting for me to give him permission to find his pleasure.

I take him deep into my mouth and nod. The first shot of his seed surprises me and I gag, but soon I'm swallowing it as if I'm drinking the sweetest wine. I keep sucking and stroking until he softens and I know I've drained him of his last drop. I lick him clean and then rest my head on his thigh.

"I love you, Angel. You are my treasure." His voice is hoarse and tired. His hand strokes my hair with a gentle touch.

He reaches down and pulls me into his lap again. We rest in each other's arms, sharing soft kisses and whispered sighs.

"Feel like a nap, love?" He sets me on my feet and helps me set my clothes to right.

"Only if it means you'll be sharing the bed with me." I fasten his trousers and grimace at the stains on his shirt.

"I hope to be sharing the bed with you for a long time to come." He kisses my cheek and takes my hand, leading me from the study.

I laugh because his bed is becoming my favorite place to be.

Part Thirty-Two

I stare at my uncle and my hands shake from nerves. He greets us with warm affection, offering drinks and a place to sit.

"My dear boy, I must say that staying with Greyson agrees with you. I've never seen you look better." He smiles at me.

"Thank you." I struggle to find the words. I glance over at the duke.

Greyson nods to encourage me, but offers no words. He's with me to support me. That is all. I must find out the full story on my own.

I brace myself and ask, "Are you helping me because you feel guilty about Jonathon?"

Uncle's face pales and shock fills his eyes. I allow him time to recover. I see pain, loss, and sadness race across his face.

"I wasn't sure you remembered him. You were so young when he died." He stares over my shoulder, lost in memories.

"I met someone yesterday who reminded me. All I really remember is leaving your house when I was ten. You and Jonathon were arguing. Two weeks later, Father informed me my cousin was dead. It was at that moment my life turned into hell." I jump to my feet and start to pace. "Did Father know about Jonathon and the groom? How could he know I'd want the same thing? I was only ten for the love of God."

Greyson reaches out and takes my hand. He pulls me down to sit next to him on the couch. His touch calms me.

"He knew about my son because in my anger and grief, I turned to him. It was a mistake. See, the uncle I received the title from was a member of your brotherhood. Your father hated him and then to find out his own nephew was a sodomite caused him to snap. He feared you turning out the same way. I guess he figured by holding you captive, he could keep you from ever encountering that sort of life. He thought he could beat the demon out of you." Remorse fills my uncle's eyes as he stares at me. "Can you forgive me? When I realized how much he'd isolated you, I tried to get you free, but everyone in your house feared him."

"I forgive you. You were the only bright spot while I was growing up. I didn't know or care if you loved me. The only thing that mattered was you didn't hate me. There was no yelling or screaming at me. You made me feel normal and I'll thank you forever for that."

We're silent for a moment. Both of us are dealing with new aspects of our relationship.

"You said you were reminded of Jonathon? How? Who would remember him?" Uncle frowns.

"I met Jonathon's lover, the groom." My uncle doesn't need to know the rest.

Uncle sits forward, resting his elbows on his knees and stares at the floor. "It took me quite a few years to forgive him. In my anger, I managed to convince myself that he was the reason why my son died. I couldn't accept my part in the tragedy. Then one morning it was as if a light came on in my head. Of all of us, the groom was the most harmed and the least to blame. He merely loved my son."

I hear the pain in my uncle's voice. I want to go to him and ease it, but only time can ease his memories.

"Jonathon and I were the ones to blame in the whole thing. My anger and fear of what society would think blinded me to the fact that I was denying my own son. Jonathon didn't have the courage to face life without me supporting him. He was afraid of being poor and having to work. That fear was stronger than any love he had for the young groom." Uncle glances up at me. "Who is he? Do you think he'd be willing to meet me so I can ask for his forgiveness?"

I shake my head. "I won't tell you who he is, Uncle. His life is his to tell, not mine. I fear he still blames you for all of it. He isn't ready to give you forgiveness."

"No, I didn't think he would be. Is he happy?" There is a need in my uncle to believe he didn't ruin Shade's life.

"He's alive, that's all I can say. I don't know if he is happy or not, but I do know he still mourns Jonathon. Maybe someday he'll remember the good in their relationship." I shrug.

"My solicitor has looked over the papers you had drawn up, making Robert your heir. They're legal and binding, so if he wishes, he can sign them." Greyson enters the conversation, trying to bury the sadness for another day.

"Good. Have you decided what you'll do, son?" Uncle leans back and relaxes.

"I have thought about it. It took a day or two to make my mind understand what you're offering. I never expected to inherit anything. To be honest, I expected to be dead by now. My father didn't seem to care whether I lived or died." I rest against Greyson. "Suddenly, I find myself free of my father and being offered a title. Plus being loved by a man the likes of which I couldn't imagine, not even in my deepest fantasies."

"A bit overwhelming, huh?" Uncle chuckles.

"Just a bit." I take Greyson's hand in mine and play with his fingers. "When I survived all those brutal beatings and my own suicide attempt, I would wonder why God wouldn't let me die. I wasn't worth anything to anyone. It made no difference if I lived or disappeared off the face of the earth. I remember begging for my father to kill me. Put me out of my misery. End my life because Hell couldn't be any worse than what I was living."

The duke lifts our entwined fingers and presses a kiss on my knuckles. "I, for one, am glad that He chose to let you stay. I'm sorry for all the pain you had to suffer, love, but things are different now. No pain. No anger. Only love."

I'm comforted by his words, even though I know there will be days when we argue. I'm tasting freedom for the first time and I have a feeling I won't meekly accept everything he expects of me. I've discovered I do have a backbone after all.

My uncle laughs again as he stands. "That's a wonderful goal to have, your grace, but it won't happen. You'll hurt each other. You'll be angry with each other. The important thing is that there will always be love between you."

We stand as well and take our leave. He escorts us to the door. "When you're ready to sign those papers, son, just let me know."

I hold out my hand to the only member of my family I respect. "Thank you, sir. I do appreciate everything you've done for me."

"It's something I should have done for my own son. You're welcome in my house any time. Both of you are." He slaps me on the back.

We climb into Greyson's carriage. I stare out the window, watching the streets go by. Greyson doesn't say anything. He seems to understand that I need to think for a moment or two.

"I wonder what I would have done in Jonathon's place?" I voice the thought racing through my head.

"Do you mean would you kill yourself if somehow we are forced apart?" Greyson takes my hand in his and rests them on his thigh.

"I guess that's what I'm asking." I lean my head back against the seat while I face him.

"My heart tells me you wouldn't. Somehow, inside you, there is a piece of steel. It won't let you break under pain or sadness. You've survived for so long, Angel. I don't see you ever giving up."

I stare down at the scars on my wrists. "I gave up once."

"That's true, but maybe God was looking out for you when your uncle found you. Maybe you were meant to live because God knew I needed you. He knew I'd love you and you'd become more important to me than anything else." He leans over and kisses me.

I bury my fingers in his hair, pressing our lips tighter together. Yes, I can believe that I am meant to love this man. Maybe God put me through Hell to allow me to enjoy Heaven even more.

Part Thirty-Three

Mist is hanging over the path as I ride along it. Greyson is in another meeting at the Home Office. My lover is exhausted. He spends most of his days at Whitehall, dealing with the prime minister and other lords in charge of the government. When he comes home, instead of resting, we make appearances at balls and soirees. Greyson knows I don't want to go to them, but he tells me we have to go because not showing our faces would make people think my father is right.

I'm not sure why we need to worry about what other people think. The duke tells me every day that he doesn't care, that he lives his life the way he wants now, yet each night we go out into Society. Maybe it is simply because I'm not used to being with people. I still get nervous and at times scared, but Alice and Harry are there with us and they help me overcome my awkwardness.

My mind drifts as I ride. Greyson told me this morning before he left that Shade has disappeared. I'm worried about the man. I fear that seeing me has driven him into a depression and he might do something irrational. I laugh at myself. If Shade has managed to stay alive and not kill himself for thirteen years, I don't think meeting me will drive him over the edge.

My heart aches for him. It can't be easy to go through life believing your love was the reason why a man killed himself. I don't think Shade is ready to understand that the blame needs to be shared between the three of them.

A noise catches my attention. As I turn around to look, a sharp pain racks my head and the world goes black.

* * * *

Pain chases me from the darkness and I open my eyes to find I'm lying in the middle of a room. My head aches, so I try not to move it too much as I glance around. It looks familiar to me. I flinch as I lift my head off the floor to get a better look.

Fear floods my mind and I whimper. Somehow I'm back in my room at my father's house. Father has made his threat come true. I start to curl in on myself, instinctively protecting my stomach. A heavy weight hampers my arms. I bring my wrist into my line of sight and groan.

Cuffs and chains. My father has captured me and I don't think he's going to let me go this time. The cold metal rubs against my wrists, reminding me that my nightmare has just begun. I close my eyes and think about Greyson.

I wonder how long it's been since I was brought here. Does Greyson know that I've been taken? Will my father brag to my lover that he's got me back? Will he tell no one, letting them all wonder where I've gone?

Another thought races through my mind. Will my father let me live? Has he kidnapped me only to kill me?

My fear increases the ache in my head and body. Lowering my head to the floor, I fight to keep a sob from bursting out. I can feel despair and hopelessness trying to take a hold of me. My bid for freedom has been in vain. I should have known that I would never escape. A perverted demon like me would never be allowed to leave Hell.

A noise brings my head up. I stare across the floor to where the door is slowly opening. I cringe, expecting to see my father standing there. I wonder when he will come. I need to be prepared for the beatings. I know he won't stop trying to whip my perversions from me.

"Edward," I gasp as my younger brother slips into the room.

"Shh." He places a finger over his lips as he glances down the hall. I assume he's making sure no one sees him entering my room.

He shuts the door with barely a noise and then makes his way to me. He's carrying a bowl and some clothes. I watch while he kneels and starts cleaning my head.

He keeps his voice low. "You have a nasty knot here. I'll try to get as much of the blood off as I can."

"Why?" I'm amazed that my brother would risk everything to help me. My father's wrath isn't something anyone in the house would wish to invoke.

"You don't deserve this. You never have. It doesn't matter what you do or who you love. He has no right to treat you no better than a dog." Edward's anger burns in his eyes.

"At least he treats his dogs better than he does his own son. They aren't chained up and beaten." I close my eyes and groan as the cool, wet cloth touches the back of my head.

"I don't have much time. He went to a ball, but I'm sure he will be coming back early to talk to you." He dips the cloth in the bowl and brushes it over my face. "He keeps the keys on him or I'd let you go. Is there anything I can do for you?"

I want to beg him to get those keys, but I'm not sure how far he's willing to go to help me. "Get a message to Uncle for me. Let him know where I am."

Edward pulls a small flask out of his pocket. He lifts my head, touching the mouth of the flask to my lips. "A little sip of whiskey should help you. Isn't there anyone else you want me to tell?"

I stare up at him as the alcohol burns down my throat into my stomach. "If you're willing to take a chance, take a message to Lord Greyson, Duke of Northampton."

I want Greyson to know where I am, though I'm sure he's figured it out by now. I have no reason to run away or disappear, not when all my dreams are coming true.

"The duke. I can do that." A soft knock breaks the silence. He gathers all his supplies and leaps to his feet. "Father's home. I'll try to come and see you when he leaves again."

"Thank you."

I watch the door close behind my younger brother. Confusion fights with the pain. Why is he helping me now? Is this a trick devised by my father to lull me into believing escape is possible?

My strength gives out and I curl up on the floor, resting my head on the cool iron cuffs. I let the darkness take me. I don't have the energy to worry about my fate. There is nothing I can do at the moment, except to try and recover. And hold to the belief that somehow Greyson will save me.

§ § § §

I don't know how long I blacked out, but when my chin hits the floor, I wake up. I stare up at the man standing in front of me. It isn't my father. I wonder who the man is.

His foot rests on the links of the chain. He has jerked my arms out from under my chin. He grins down at me and I shiver at the evil gleam in his eyes.

"Lord Williamson tells me you are in need of purification."

My gaze skates over his body and I can feel my face show my shock when my eyes get to the white collar the man is wearing. Oh my God. This man is a priest. Sweat beads on my forehead and my mouth goes dry.

He reaches down, grabbing the collar of my shirt, and jerks me up so that our noses are almost touching. He growls and I see the madness lurking in his dark eyes. Every part of me wants to run and hide. I fear what this man will do to me.

The priest shakes me like a dog with a fox. "I've seen you and that sodomite together. It's a good thing your father called me. You still might be saved from eternal damnation, but it will take work. It will take blood and tears. Your salvation is yours if only you denounce the perversions burning in your demonic heart."

I keep my mouth shut. My mind urges me to do what he says. It tells me to open my mouth and give voice to the lies he wants me to spout. It reminds me of the agony from the whip cutting in to my flesh. I don't want to feel the weight of the leather on my skin. I can't stand to hear the whistle of the cane in the air.

The scars on my back tighten and I remember that promises mean nothing. I've begged for forgiveness before and paid with a pound of my flesh. Yet mercy was never given. My heart understands that denouncing the perversions means denying the man I love, and my soul isn't willing to base its salvation on that.

My silence seems to enrage him. He shakes me again. "You'll be begging for forgiveness when I'm done with you. You'll turn away from the Devil's ways and embrace the ways of the redeemed." A tender look from him causes my stomach to roll. "I know what it's like to be tempted by the Devil and find your will is weak. I allowed the Devil to be scourged from my soul. Your father is going to let me save your soul and then we will go after the demon who tempted you away from the path."

"No," I say through gritted teeth. "I'll never ask forgiveness from you or my father. I've done nothing wrong."

I never see his hand coming. It collides with my cheek, flinging my head back. I try not to cry out. The strength Greyson believes I have is flooding me. I will never give them the satisfaction of hearing me beg.

He drops me back on the floor and kicks me. I bite through my lip to keep the moan of pain in. I'll be strong. I'll hold out as long as I can because I know that Greyson will come for me. He won't allow me to stay in my father's hands for long. But I won't sit still waiting to be rescued. I might just be able to free myself, but whether I'm rescued or whether I die at my father's hands, it won't be as a cowering dog. I won't fear him anymore.

I let the darkness take me again. There has been enough defiance today.

Part Thirty-Four

"Wake up."

The order breaks through the blackness clouding my mind. I moan to myself as I roll over and push myself to a sitting position. I force my gaze to meet my father's. It is difficult since he has often punished me for daring to look him in the eye.

His grin is filled with pride. "I told you I would have you back," he gloated.

"Yes. It seems that you were right for once." Surprise ripples through me. Who is speaking? The boy I was would never challenge his father like that. The child knows the consequences of defiance.

He hisses and slaps me. "Don't talk back, boy. I'm your father and I own you."

"You don't own me. You've never owned me. All you've done is held me captive and abused me because of your own fears and ignorance." I find I have the strength to climb to my feet.

When I gain my feet, I see a flash of fear shoot through my father's eyes. It is in that moment, I realize I'm taller than my father. For so long, he has played the role of the Devil in my nightmares. In those nightmares, my father was a monster, invincible and powerful. In the light of day, I see that he is old and small. His power over me lessens even more. He may hold me chained to this room, but he no longer controls my fear.

I stare at my father and I can tell he's beginning to understand that I'll no longer cower before him. He's losing some of his confidence. He's filled with doubt.

"I know what freedom is. I'm not a monster, Father. You are." The conviction of my own father's guilt fills me. None of it has been my fault.

"Demon." A hand grabs my collar and pushes me to my knees. It's the priest from earlier today. I see the passion in his eyes and I understand his passion is for the agony he'll be causing me.

The priest holds a whip in his hand. I don't look at the black strip of leather. I know what it can do and the suffering it can cause. That instrument of evil has touched me too many times to forget.

My first reaction is to tense, but I've decided I'll take whatever punishment they feel fit to give me. They're the evil ones, not me. They are the ones who take perverse joy in causing pain. Father moves to the other side of the room. The priest forces me to the floor, unchaining my cuffs from the ring they're locked in. He tears my shirt so it hangs down around my waist and gathers at my wrists.

A crack breaks the air and my back begins to ache before the first blow lands. I know what is to come. I bow my head and spread my arms out, offering myself up to their hatred. I can endure this. I've survived thirteen years. I can take a few more hours or days. I've been free. I will be free again.

As the leather bites deep into my flesh for the first time, I swallow my scream. I allow my mind to bring an image of Greyson before my gaze. His brilliant blue eyes fill with the love he holds for me. Fire burns over my back as another lash cuts into my skin. By the time I'm free, I'll have scars on my scars, but I don't think about that right now. I focus on the feel of Greyson's arms around me. My back straightens and I lift my head to stare at my father. Just thinking of my lover gives me the courage to accept the whipping.

I know from experience that I will go numb after a while. The body can only take so much pain before the mind shuts down. Warm liquid trickles down my back and soaks into the waistband of my trousers. Another stripe is added to my lower back. This one cuts deep and I can feel it in my spine.

A sob lodges in my throat. I won't beg. I won't plead. I will continue to love Greyson with all of my soul and I'll never deny what my heart says is right. The whipping continues and my mind slowly distances itself from my body.

My father says something to me, but I can't hear his words. I'm remembering each moment with Greyson in my soul. As each touch and kiss takes away the pain, I realize that I've never once spoken of my love for the duke. I never told Greyson how much I love him.

The shock rippling through me has nothing to do with the leather marking my back. It comes from my heart. Why have I never told the duke how much I love him? Why haven't I uttered anything to let Greyson know that my world ceases to exist without him?

A slap to the face brings my attention back to my father. He screams at me, but again I can't hear the words. Spittle hits my cheek and I understand that this is why I never said I love you to Greyson. Deep inside me, I never really believed I'd be free of my father. I know his reach is long and the chains with which I was bound to Father were strong. Maybe by not saying the words, I thought I would keep myself from falling apart when I returned to hell.

Yet here I kneel, bleeding and tortured, but not begging. Not asking forgiveness for a love so perfect that even if the Devil sent it, I'd accept it with open arms. I promise myself as soon as I am free, I'll tell Greyson about my love.

"Whom do you belong to?" My father slaps me again and I realize the whipping has stopped for the moment.

The priest drags me to my feet and then moves to stand beside my father. "Do you belong to the Devil, child?"

"Yes, I do." I nod towards the man whose name I bear. "If he insists that I am his, then yes, I belong to the Devil."

"No, I'm your father. I gave you life." Father moves towards me, raising his hand to strike at me again.

The priest shrugs. "Answer his question, son. Whom do you belong to?"

Part Thirty-Five

Whom do I belong to? I know what he wants me to say. It is a game he likes to play. Before this moment I would have said what he wanted to hear, if only to try and get a reprieve from the beating. It never worked and this time I know the true answer to his question.

"Whom do you belong to?" He screams again. The priest grabs my hair at the back of my head and jerks back hard enough to make my neck hurt.

"I belong to no one." My words are forced between gritted teeth. My back throbs with pain as blood pours down from my wounds.

"You belong to me. You carry my name. You're mine." Father's face flushes red and I see the fury building in him.

"If I belong to anyone, it would be Lord Greyson. I'm not your son. I am Greyson's lover." These words might push him over the edge, but they are my truth.

"Pervert! That sodomite has seduced you into believing perversion is love. What is your name?" This is another game he plays with me, having me repeat my name over and over. He is reinforcing the idea that I belong to him since our names are the same.

I stare at him and grin through my pain. "My name is Angel."

Rage takes hold of him and his fist rams into my face. I feel my head snap back and my nose break. My knees start to buckle. I tense. There is no way I'll allow myself to fall to my knees in front of my father. When I kneel again, it will be without pain and only to bring pleasure or comfort. I glare defiantly at him, blood dripping from my chin.

"Hit me," I challenge him. I wave a weak hand towards the man holding me. "Beat me." I scrub my hand over the blood on my face and hold it out towards my father. "Spill my blood until it pools beneath me. I'll never deny my love or my lover."

Shock pushes through the anger in my father's eyes. He steps away from my hand.

"I no longer fear you." I throw back my shoulders and straighten so I'm standing taller than he is. My body screams in agony. Pain is beginning to return. "I pity you. You live in fear and face the world with anger. You'll never know love from anyone, not even your own family. At least while I'm burning in Hell for my perversions, I'll know I'm loved."

I take a shallow breath. That's all my battered body will allow. I look for the whip the man dropped. I spot it and make my way slowly over to it. Bending is torture. I'm afraid I'll fall over, but I grasp the handle. I hand it to the priest. After I make sure he holds it, I turn and offer my back to him.

"Take a pound of flesh, Father. Try to beat the demons from me. Kill me if that's the only way you know of to drive this disease from me. It matters little to me what you think. I love Lord Greyson, and I'll die loving him."

In that instance with those words still ringing through the air, I feel the last chain holding my heart captive break. Fear flees before the truth I've spoken. In the love I have for Greyson, I've found the ability to love myself. No one will ever be able to make me believe I'm a monster because I love a man. No opinion will matter to me so much that I lose myself.

The man with the whip growls and I hear the leather whistle through the air. Pain rips through my body, but I accept it. I no longer fight it, not even when my legs give out and I fall to my knees. For my brain has taken the suffering away and all I can see before me is Greyson smiling and loving me.

A knock interrupts the beating. Father walks to the door while he gestures for the man to stop. "What is it? I said I didn't want to be disturbed." He yanks open the door.

A nervous footman shifts from side to side. "My lord, the Duke of Northampton and the Earl are here. We told them you were unavailable, but they demand your presence."

Relief surges through me. Edward kept his promise and they came. I manage a chuckle. "I told you I'd be free again."

"That's what you think. Come with me." He heads out of the room with the stranger behind him. "Keep an eye on that one and make sure he doesn't get out," Father orders the footman.

"Yes, my lord." The servant bows his head, but I see his gaze dart over to me.

Disgust fills the young footman's face after my father disappears down the hall. The servant moves towards me and I find myself tensing, expecting him to hit me.

"Bastard."

The hate-filled words surprise me. I glance up at him and see he's staring at the slices across my back. I want to shrug my shoulders to show I don't care what he thinks, but the pain is too much. I struggle to get to my feet.

"Don't move, my lord." The footman touches my shoulder. "Master Edward will be here in a second. He'll help you."

"Shouldn't," is all I'm able to force out.

"I turned my back for too long, brother." Edward enters the room. He has a shirt over his arm. He hands it to the footman. "James, hold on to this. I'll get Robert up and we can cover him with that."

"Angel," I hiss, his hands bracing me as I push myself off the floor.

"Right." He manages to work the remnants off my wrists.

"I have this." James holds up a small key.

"Good man." Edward grabs it and frees me from the cold iron cuffs.

"You shouldn't help me. If he knows you did it, he'll punish you." I wobble, trying to pull the clean shirt on.

Edward tugs it over my head and gently lays it over the wounds on my back. I can tell the fabric is soaking up the blood.

"He won't. We'll help you to the stairs and then we disappear.

James has already been fired, though Father doesn't remember he did it. So it doesn't matter for him." He lets me lean on him as we make our way down the hallway to the stairs.

I study the stairway. It's the pathway to my permanent freedom, but I don't know if my body has the strength to move.

"Where is Robert, Williamson? I demand to see him. I won't leave without him." Greyson's voice drifts up to where we stood on the landing.

My love is down there and I'm not willing to wait any longer to be with him again. I take the first step towards true freedom. Before I go any further, I turn back to look at my brother.

"Why?"

"One of us should be free to live our life the way we want. He's punished you for years for no real reason. I used to stand outside the door and listen to him beat you. Tears would roll down my cheeks when you cried and begged for him to stop." Edward stops and swallows, blinking back tears. "It wasn't fair that he took his fear out on you. It wasn't fair that I got everything while you barely survived."

Greyson's voice breezes up to us again. "Williamson, Robert is my lover. I'm not ashamed to admit that. I won't leave him to suffer at your hands anymore."

"You've found someone to love and who loves you. You deserve the chance to live, Angel." Edward smiles at me. "Now, go before the duke kills Father."

"If either of you ever need anything, come to me. I promise I'll help."

I turn and begin making my way down the stairs, each step one of piercing agony and uplifting joy.

Part Thirty-Six

"You seduced my son and have perverted his immortal soul with your evil ways. He'll be dead before I let you have him back."

I lean against the doorframe, staring into the drawing room where my father and Greyson stand, face-to-face. Father is gesturing wildly, his anger turning his face beet red. Greyson's eyes are as hard and cold as diamonds. He doesn't move as my father pokes a finger at his chest.

"You were killing him anyway. All I did is love him and give him a normal life. I didn't hold him captive or chain him in a room. I didn't take everything away from him. Unlike you, I know how to love someone and treat him like a person." Greyson steps closer to Father. "If you've harmed him in any way, I'll kill you where you stand."

I know the threat is real. As much as I've always dreamed of my father dying, I don't want my lover to be the one who kills him. "Greyson."

My soft voice explodes in the room. Everyone turns to look at me. Father's eyes are filled with fear and anger. My uncle's face holds relief. Greyson stares at me, tears making his eyes shine.

"Angel," he whispers, taking a step towards me.

I straighten up and try to move to him, but my strength disappears. My knees buckle, but Greyson cradles me in his arms before I hit the floor. His arms wrap around me tight. I cry out as he presses against my back. He frowns, touching my face lightly with his fingers. The duke helps me sit up and then glances at my back.

In a flash, he's on his feet and stalking towards my father. Without hesitating, he hits Father in the face with his fist. My uncle comes and kneels beside me. I try to say something, anything to make Greyson stop beating my father.

Tears roll down my cheeks. I'm tired of the anger and

violence. I want to go home. I want to curl up in our bed and with Greyson's arms around me. I need to feel safe.

"No." I moan, trying to climb to my feet. "No more."

Uncle holds me down. "Don't move. Greyson, get your ass over here. Angel needs you."

Greyson pulls away from my father and races across the floor to me. He joins me on the floor, reaching out to touch my face and my chest. He's seen the blood and I think he's afraid that by touching me, he'll cause me more pain.

"Oh, my beautiful Angel. How can I help you?" His voice breaks and tears stream down his face.

I lean forward, even as my back protests any movement and bring our lips together. It's a gentle kiss, full of promise and healing.

I pull back enough to say, "I love you."

His hands cup my face and he rests his forehead against mine. "You love me."

"Yes. I'm sorry I didn't say it before this. I'm sorry I was too scared to trust in myself." I place my trembling hand over his chest where his heart beat, strong and true.

"Never be sorry, Angel. You love me." He gathers me in a soft embrace as if he held a baby bird and lifts me up. A sharp groan explodes from me. He looks down with a worried frown. "I'll try not to hurt you, my love." He moves slow, not jostling my body the best he can.

"No matter what you do, I'll hurt. Just take me home." I rest my head on his shoulder.

"I'll do that, love." He glances at my uncle. "Take care of this."

"Certainly, your grace." My uncle brushes a hand over my shoulder. "I'll see you in a day or two."

"Thank you." I smile as best I can through the pain.

A movement catches my eye and I see my brother standing

at the top of the stairs. He nods and I know I'll be seeing him again. There is nothing to be envied about being Father's heir. I've discovered we might not be able to choose our relatives, but we can choose our family.

I believe my brother will reach a moment when he realizes he has nothing to lose as well. When he comes to me, I will receive him with open arms and no anger. We all do what we must to survive.

"You are the spawn of the Devil." The priest stands before us. His eyes gleam with a fanatic light. He points a trembling hand at us.

"You are a hypocrite, Father." Greyson glares at the man while he moves towards the priest. "How many children have you punished for your own sins? How many suffer because of the temptations you succumb to every day?"

The preacher flinches and takes a step back. "I don't know what you're talking about."

"You do know and so does the Archbishop. I think you should expect a visit from him soon." Greyson shoulders the man aside. "Get out of my way."

We make our way outside and settle into the carriage. I press my face above Greyson's shirt and against his warm scent. I breathe as deep as my ribs will allow, taking in his scent. I'm safe. My heart, mind and body know it.

"Oh love, I'm sorry. I'm so sorry." Greyson's whispers bath my ear as his hands try to find a place to touch me without hurting me.

"No. It's not your fault. It's my father's." I'm keeping the pain at bay by thinking of Greyson's hands touching me with love.

"I should have known he'd try something like this. I should have kept you safe."

I can hear guilt and sorrow tainting his voice. I brace against the pain and lean back to look at him. I shake my head, touching his face with my hand.

"You kept me safe by giving me freedom. The only way you could have kept me from my father is by locking me away in your house. You wouldn't do that to me." I brush a kiss over his lips. "You gave me freedom and in doing that, you taught me to be strong. That's why I'm not afraid of him anymore. I knew you were coming."

"I can't explain how I felt when that footman showed up to tell me your father had kidnapped you. I was afraid you'd be dead by the time I got there."

Tears stream down his face and wash the blood from mine.

"I'm alive. I'm alive, Greyson. I love you and nothing is going to keep me from proving that to you every day of our lives together."

Our fingers entwine and rest between our chests, feeling our hearts beat as one. I rest my head against his shoulder and let the rhythm soothe me.

Part Thirty-Seven

I'm roused from my pain-induced stupor when Greyson hands me to a footman so the duke can climb out of the carriage. Greyson enfolds me in his arms again and moves into the house, calling for Johnson, the butler and the housekeeper.

They convene in our bedroom. Greyson lays me on my stomach in the middle of the bed. I don't know who sobs, but I'm sure my back isn't a pretty sight. I manage to move my head, so I can see them.

"Have a footman go for the doctor," Greyson orders the butler. From the housekeeper, he asks for warm water and sheets torn into bandages. "We'll have to soak your shirt off, love. It's dried to the wounds."

"It's happened before." Quite a few times, but I'm not interested in telling those stories. I close my eyes to rest.

§ § § §

"Love, the doctor's here." Greyson's voice and touch on my shoulder wake me up.

I find I'm naked with a sheet covering me from the waist down. I must have lost consciousness since I never felt them cleaning or moving me.

"Fine."

I close my eyes again. Greyson's hand trails down my arm to grasp my hand. The mattress dips a little and I peek through half open eyes to see the duke sitting next to me. I squeeze his hand each time the doctor probes a deep wound.

Finally the doctor finishes with my back. He takes a quick glance at my nose. He rinses his hands after bandaging my torn flesh.

"Some of the wounds are deep, so I'd keep an eye on them. They might fester. You'll get a fever. We'll deal with that when it comes. The best I can tell you, my lord, is you'll heal, but it'll take a while and you'll have more scars to add to your collection." The doctor frowns. "I'll be back tomorrow to check on you." He nods to both of us and Johnson escorts him out.

Greyson moves from the bed to a chair set beside it. He's farther away than I like, but he reaches out to take my hand.

"What did he do to you, love?" His voice is broken and fills with sorrow.

"He freed me, Greyson." My voice is hoarse from exhaustion and pain.

A puzzled frown appears on Greyson's face. "He put you in chains and whipped you until your back looks like raw meat." He caresses my palm. "How does this free you?"

"I no longer fear him. I no longer hate myself. I understand what love is and I'm strong enough to embrace it when I see it." I bring his hand to my mouth and kiss it. "He has no power over me anymore. I'm free."

"What happened?"

I shake my head. I'm not ready to tell Greyson about my ordeal. Maybe I never will. "When we left Father's house, you told Uncle to take care of him. How will he do that?"

Greyson let me change the subject. Maybe in his heart, he knows he isn't ready to hear it. "It seems your father owes a few men quite a bit of money. So between your uncle and I, we bought the markers. As long as he leaves us alone and quits spreading rumors, we won't call in the debts. The minute he tries anything, we send him to debtor's prison."

"Will it work?" I'm fighting to stay awake.

He squeezes my hand and smiles. "Rest now. I'll be here when you wake up. You're home."

I allow my eyes to drift shut. For the first time I believe it's true. I am safe and I'm home. I've faced my demons and become stronger because of it. Greyson's hand grasps mine until I fall asleep.

§ § § §

When I open my eyes next, Greyson is still sitting in the chair, sleeping with his head resting against the back. I stare at my lover and wonder how I have gotten so lucky. The priest would say it is the Devil's own luck, but I have a feeling that this is a gift. A gift I'm more than ready to accept.

I shift and pain shoots through me. My sharp intake of breath wakes him. He smiles when he sees I'm watching him. He leans forward, touching my shoulder with gentle fingers.

"Are you all right, love?"

"I'm fine but you are too far away, I think." I manage to form my bruised face into a smile.

"I long to hold you in my arms and prove to myself that you're here and safe, but I'm afraid of hurting you." He slides from the chair and kneels beside the bed. His lips meet mine in a soft kiss.

I open up to him, encouraging him to take the kiss deeper. He doesn't and when my face begins to ache, I'm glad he chooses to keep it light. He pulls back, but I grab his hand.

"Please lie next to me, Greyson. I need to feel your warmth. I've felt worse pain. You can't hurt me." I tug on his hand.

He stares at me for a moment then stands. He strips off his waistcoat and shirt. His shoes join the pile. He leaves his pants on and climbs on the bed, staying on top of the sheet. As soon as he's settled, I slide over and lay my head on his chest. One of his hands comes to rest on the swell of my buttocks. His other hand strokes the hair at the nape of my neck.

We both sigh. This embrace is what we need to reassure our hearts that we're still together and safe. His lips brush my hair and I feel him relax.

"Your uncle had to stop me from killing your father," he admits to me in a quiet voice.

"Uncle's a smart man. Violence wouldn't have solved anything. You would have had to leave the country. What would your sons have done?" I shift, pressing closer to him. "I'm sure they need you."

"I've not been a wonderful father, Angel. They have been neglected, but not to the extent I ignored their mother."

"You can change that. When I'm feeling better, you should go and visit with them. Let them know you care for them." I move to look up at him. "You can repair the damage caused by neglect. With love and attention, your sons will begin to open their hearts to you."

He doesn't say anything for a moment. "When you are healed and the doctor says you can travel, we'll go visit them."

My surprise must have shown in my eyes because he chuckles. "They are old enough to meet you as a friend, but I'll wait awhile before I tell them anything else."

"Eventually they will figure us out, but you're right. For now, it's best if they think of me as a friend of yours." I lay my head back down on his shoulder. "I'll show them how much you love them, even when it didn't seem like you did."

"Who better than you to know the difference between neglect and abuse?" His hand caresses my lower back and my buttocks.

My body decides it's tired and time for me to rest again. "Stay," I whisper against his skin.

"Until you want me to leave." He holds me close.

I want to tell him I'll need him with me forever, but sleep claims me and I drift down into my dreams.

LIFE BEGINS

Part One

One week later...

I'm reading in our bed. It's a little past midnight. Greyson has gone to another in a long line of endless balls. It has been a week and I'm still recovering from my ordeal with my father. So I've chosen to stay home. My back is painful enough that dancing makes it nearly impossible for me to move the next day.

The door opens and Shade slips in. I set my book aside with a frown. Greyson has told me he hasn't been in touch with the other man since he left our house in tears that day. Shade stands just inside the closed door and stares at me.

Without thought, I hold out my hand to him. That must be the gesture he's waiting for since he comes and takes my hand in his. I tug to get him to sit next to me on the bed. He sits but doesn't look at me. The candlelight flickers in his green eyes as his gaze studies my hand.

"Where have you been?" I ask in a soft voice. I don't want to startle him.

"I've been away." His growl is harsh but gentle.

"We've been worried about you." I brush my thumb over the knuckles on his hand.

His eyes skate towards me as if he's surprised anyone would worry about him. "Greyson knows I disappear from time to time."

"Yes and he's tried telling me that you would be okay, but I'm afraid I still worried about you." I smile and risk touching his cheek with my fingers. There's a fragile air surrounding him. One wrong touch and he will shatter.

He doesn't pull away from me, but his gaze returns to our linked hands. "I went to Jonathon's grave. Had to sneak onto the grounds."

"Would you like permission to visit whenever you want to?" I long to give this lonely man one gift.

An incredulous snort comes from him. "Your uncle will never allow me to step foot on his property. I don't want you to risk his wrath by asking for me."

Chuckling, I grip Shade's square chin and turn it so his eyes meet mine. "I don't have to ask my uncle, though I know he would say yes. I'm his heir now and as such I can give you the permission you need."

"His heir? Why would he make you his heir when he would have disowned Jonathon if my love had lived?" Anger and confusion war in his eyes.

"Uncle knows the mistakes he made all those years ago, Shade. He knows that he wronged not only Jonathon but you as well. Maybe if Jonathon had held out, Uncle would have changed his mind. Maybe not." I shrug. "We'll never know for sure. Yet Uncle has stood beside me in my bid for freedom from my father. He's never once spoken out against Greyson and I being together. All he's ever asked is that I make sure this is what I want because our lives will be hard and society will not be overly kind to us."

"You trust him?" Shade nuzzles into my hand.

In some ways, it is strange touching another man like I touch Greyson. Yet I know my lover wouldn't be upset about this. "Not as much as I trust Greyson, but my uncle has always been there for me when I needed him. When I tried to kill myself, he saved me and made sure I was taken care of. It's another way to atone for his own son's death. I believe he means it when he says he's sorry for what he did."

His eyes fill with tears as he looks at me. I wonder if he is seeing me or if he's seeing his long-gone lover. Leaning forward, I whisper a kiss over his lips and decide it doesn't matter. He is hurting and lost in his own way like I was before I met Greyson.

Diamond drops of water roll down his cheeks. I touch a fingertip to one and bring the wetness to my lips. Tasting the saltiness of his pain, I wrap my arms around his shoulders and urge him to lie beside me in the bed. He doesn't argue or struggle as I tuck him under the blankets and cradle him against my body.

I hold him tight as sobs wrack his lean frame. My hands rub his back and I murmur soothing words. Years of pain flow from his eyes. I fear saying or doing the wrong thing. Shade is close to shattering and I don't want to push him over the edge. So I let him cry.

After several minutes, a shudder racks his body and he sighs. My nightshirt is drenched, but I don't mind. He rolls over to his back and stares up at the ceiling. Wiping his face with one hand, he reaches for mine with his other.

"Thank you, Angel." His growls attest to the roughness of his throat from the sobs.

"You're welcome." I don't say anything else because there is a hint of shame on his face. "It's not weak to cry for someone you've lost. Anyway, it's only me who knows and I promise not to tell anyone."

He gives me a weak smile. I lie on my side and look down at him. Brushing his hair from his forehead, I kiss his cheek. He squeezes my hand.

"Tell me about Jonathon," I ask in a hesitant voice. I'm not sure he's ready to talk about my cousin, but I know it would ease his grief even more by remembering the good times.

The memories come in bits and pieces until his voice fades and he falls asleep. I blow out the candle and pull the blankets up around us. I whisper a prayer into the darkness. I pray that this haunted man finds peace with his past. He rolls to his side and I snuggle up behind him. He takes our entwined hands and places them over his heart. I say another prayer. I hope Shade finds someone to love and lets go of the pain my cousin caused him. I feel his heart beat slow as I fall asleep.

Part Two

I'm being held against a warm chest when I wake up. I snuggle closer. Greyson's familiar scent fills my nose and I frown. Peeking up through my lashes, I meet his blue gaze. Turning my head, I glance to the other side of the bed. Shade is gone.

"He left just after dawn." Greyson's voice rumbles under my ear.

"I hope he is well," I murmur, not interested in climbing out of bed.

"I think he will be. How did he come to be sharing our bed?" There is no anger or accusation in his voice.

I rub my thumb over his lips and lean in to give him a quick kiss. Restlessness hits me and I climb out from under the covers. Stretching, I go to stand by the window. I pull one of the curtains back and stare out over the garden.

"He arrived here late last night. I was reading. I told him I was worried about him. He seemed surprised by that." I shoot my lover a quick glance. "He doesn't have anyone who cares about him."

"He has you and me now." Greyson pushes up so that he can lean against the headboard.

Nodding, I look back outside. "He went to visit Jonathon's grave. He had to sneak onto the estate. I told him he had my permission to go whenever he wanted. Then we talked about my cousin and fell asleep." I don't mention Shade's tears. Crying is a private matter best kept between him and me. I don't think Shade would want to look weak in front of Greyson.

"He was curled up in your arms when I got home."

I tense. Again there is no anger in his voice, but I can't help thinking I did something wrong. "Are you angry?" I ask in a soft voice.

"No, love. I trust you." Greyson yawns.

"I kissed him." I feel as if I'm confessing to murder.

"Did you enjoy it?" Greyson gets out of bed and joins me at the window. Encircling my waist with his arms, he pulls me back against him.

"I did it to try and ease his pain. It was nothing like our kisses." I lean my head on his shoulder and listen to his steady breathing.

"I didn't think it was." He turns me to face him. Cupping my chin in his hands, he stares down at me. "I'm not angry with you. You have a good heart, love."

I kiss him. Our lips move together in a waltz, touching and teasing. I love his taste. No one else will ever make me feel like he does. He leads me back to bed where we hold each other close under the covers.

"Do you think I've helped him?" I trace a pattern over Greyson's chest.

"If anyone could, it would be you. You remind him of his lost love and even though they are faded, you have memories of Jonathon as well." His hand slides down my back and rests on the swell of my ass.

"Maybe someday he will meet my uncle and they can remember my cousin together," I whisper against his throat.

"It's a possibility." His lips trail over my ear to nibble on the skin behind it.

I moan. "I want you to make love to me. I need to feel you inside me."

"You're still recovering, Angel. I don't want to hurt you." Worry wars with lust in his eyes.

"You could never hurt me. I trust you." I rub my hand over his prick.

"You're too tempting for your own good, love."

He pushes pillows behind his back. Soon he's sitting up and I'm straddling him, my thighs resting against his hips. My favorite little jar is plucked from the nightstand and he pours oil over his fingers.

"Brace your hands on my shoulders. I'll get you ready to ride me." He places a hard kiss on my mouth. "It's the only way to ensure the wounds on your back aren't bothered."

My forehead drops forward to rest on his chest as his fingers trace the crease of my buttocks. I can't stop the moan as he grazes my opening with his fingertips. I want him to make love to me without worrying about hurting me. My heart needs reassurance that I really do belong to him. Pressure builds as he slides one finger in. I tilt my hips, asking for more.

One finger becomes two and then three. Greyson kisses me, his tongue mimicking the actions of his fingers. I find myself rocking back, working his fingers deeper inside me. His knuckles brush the sweet spot I've grown to appreciate.

"Ah." A sound bursts from me as sparks shoot through my body. My gaze meets his and I ask, "Come inside, love?"

He nods and I moan as his fingers leave me empty. The jar is opened and the oil dipped out. I look over my shoulder to watch him cover his shaft with the slick liquid. His hands move to my hips and he encourages me to rise to my knees. I close my eyes, allowing him to guide me. I shiver as the blunt head of his prick bumps my opening.

"Easy. Just take it slow." His warm breath bathes my ear as I lower myself on to him. Taking my time, I soon impale myself.

I tighten my channel, massaging his prick in my own way. His head falls back against the headboard. I rise up and drop back down, riding him with tender strokes. The blue fire of his eyes warms me as much as the passion racing through my body. His grip on my hips tightens to the point where I know I'll have bruises tomorrow. Our movements become faster and harder. The sound of our flesh coming together excites me as much as the moans and groans coming from my lover's throat.

"Angel." Greyson pries one hand off my hip and wraps it around my shaft. He pumps once, then a second time and I'm coming. My seed coats his hand, stomach and chest. I know the smell and sound of my completion drives the duke over the edge. He slams up into me. His seed spills in me, wet and warm. It's the warmth I feel the most. It seems to follow through me, burning away all the cold and empty places left in my body, filling it with his love.

I collapse on his chest and lie there, trying to catch my breath. His hands trace the patterns of my scars without truly touching them. He kisses the top of my head as he sets me on my side next to him. I have no energy to protest when he climbs from the bed to grab a cloth.

"We still have a little time before we really need to start our morning. I think a snuggle under the blankets sounds like a good idea." He settles down beside me after cleaning us.

A knock sounds and Johnson sticks his head around the door. "Your Grace, Lord Thompson from the Home Office is waiting downstairs in your study."

Greyson sighs. "Okay, Johnson. Tell him I'll be down in a few minutes."

"Certainly, your grace." The valet closes the door.

I pout as the duke climbs out of bed. He laughs and I can't help but smile as he gets dressed. I sit up with the covers pooled around my waist when he comes to give me a kiss.

"Are you going to lounge around bed all day?" He brushes his lips over mine.

I shake my head, causing our mouths to rub together. He moans and pulls me closer. Soon I'm straddling his lap and we're rocking together. Before we get too far, he breaks our kiss and dumps me back on to the mattress.

"You're trying to distract me, love. I can't keep Thompson waiting any longer." He growls at me.

I laugh. "Honest, I wasn't." I bound from the bed, ignoring the fact that I'm nude. In the weeks that I've been with Greyson, I've been slowly accepting my body, scars and all. Opening the dressing room, I turn to find him watching me with lust in his eyes. "I'm going to go riding. If you get finished with Lord Thompson before I get back, come and find me. If not, I'll see you when I return."

He comes to me and places his hands on my arms. Looking down into my eyes, he asks, "You aren't worried about your father kidnapping you again?"

I want to give him a light joking answer, but then I stop and think about his question. "Not anymore. I don't think he'll try it again. I no longer fear him and that was the only power he had over me." The hate and anger I usually feel when talking about my father is gone. It left the night I walked out of his house and back into Greyson's arms.

"Good." He gives me a hard kiss and then heads out of the room. "I'll find you when I'm finished."

"All right." I get dressed and make my way down to the front hall where the butler stands with my coat, hat and gloves.

As I mount my gelding, I have the urge to go and talk to my uncle. I tell the footman, "Let his grace know that I've gone to see my uncle."

"Certainly, my lord." The young man bows as I ride away.

§ § § §

"My dear boy, it's great to have you come and visit. Unfortunately, your cousin isn't up yet. I'm sure she'll be unhappy to hear she missed you." Uncle greets me with a firm handshake. "You'll join me for breakfast, won't you?"

"I'd love to, sir." I follow him into his breakfast room. "I'll make it a point to stop by later when she is receiving."

"She'll like that. My daughter doesn't have much regard for the rest of your family." Uncle nods and lets the footmen serve us.

"I feel the same way." I wait until the footmen are done and have retreated to the corners of the room. "Uncle, I saw Shade again last night."

He frowns. "Shade?"

"Yes, Jonathon's love." I wonder for a moment if this is the right thing to do.

"Oh, the young groom." Uncle nods. "I'm glad he's come back. I know you were worried about him."

"Yes. He told me he sneaks onto your property to go and visit Jonathon's grave. I hope you don't mind, but I gave him permission to visit there any time he wants without worrying about getting in trouble." I fight the urge to duck my head and apologize for giving anyone permission.

"That's fine. You're my heir now. You can do pretty much whatever you'd like with my property, son. It's about time this Shade and I learn to forgive each other. I'll make sure my estate manager knows." Uncle settles back in his chair. "So tell me about your encounter with your father."

For the next hour, I discuss my father and other things with my uncle. There are still things I don't tell him. Things I haven't spoken of with Greyson either. Maybe someday those wounds will heal and I can speak of them.

I find that it's nice to have someone to talk to about everything, including my relationship with Greyson. Finally, I decide I really do want to go riding. As I'm taking my leave of my Uncle, he orders his mount and joins me.

Heading out to Hyde Park, we laugh and talk. I find myself wishing I had gotten a chance to know my uncle sooner. He might have made my life a little less miserable.

Part Three

When I arrive home, I find Greyson's servants in an uproar. The duke stands calmly in the maelstrom, barking out orders. One of the footmen rushes over to take my coat and hat. Walking over to where Greyson stands, I tug off my gloves and toss them on a table.

"What is all the fuss about?" I touch his hand to get his attention.

Turning, he brushes a small kiss over my cheek. I blush. I'm still not totally comfortable with displays of affection in front of his servants. He shakes his head and laughs.

"We're going to France." He waves another footman over and hands him a piece of paper. "Take this note to Roberts."

"Yes, your grace." The footman runs off.

"France? Why would we do that?" I'm puzzled. Greyson hadn't said anything about taking a trip.

"While the past couple of weeks have been the best weeks of my life, they have also been the most exhausting. I think we need some time away from London." He places his hand at the small of my back and leads me towards his study.

"If getting out of London is what you want, can't we just go to one of our country estates? I thought you said traveling on the Continent is getting dangerous." I sit in the chair he gestures to and watch while he pours us both a drink. "Little early in the day to be drinking, isn't it? Greyson, what's going on?"

He hands me my glass and goes to stare out the window. "One of the reasons why Shade stopped by last night was to leave me some information. The rumors about Napoleon are getting worse. He couldn't get anything concrete about them because he doesn't move in the same circles."

I take a sip of the whiskey and then say, "But you can move in the right part of society to be able to find out for certain if those rumors were true."

He nods. "So Thompson wants me to take an extended trip to Paris and see what I can find out."

"Ah." I'm not sure how I feel about that. He makes his way over to me and kneels in front of me.

"I figured you and I could go. Get away from here for a while." His warm hand presses my thigh.

"You'd want me to go with you? I'm still not comfortable in Society." Comfortable? I laugh silently. I can barely say three words when I'm in a crowd of strangers.

"Yes, I want you to go with me. I love you, Angel. I'll always want you with me, no matter where I go. I told Johnson to pack your things as well. Your mount will be taken to my country estate until we get back." He squeezes my knee and stands as if I've already said yes.

"Wait. I didn't say I'd go. What about my uncle? What about my responsibilities to him?" I admit the thought of not seeing Greyson for months terrifies me, but I can't just throw everything else in my life to the wind when he tells me to.

Frowning, he glances at me. "Now isn't the time to be stubborn, love. We must leave as soon as possible."

"I'm not being stubborn, Greyson." I stand and set my glass down on his desk. "I'm trying to make up my own mind. Shouldn't I be allowed to decide for myself whether or not I wish to risk my life? I didn't sign any paper that says I'll spy for my country. That was you and I didn't realize that by loving you, I'd be included in this deal." I'm forcing down the anger and hurt.

"Don't you want to be with me?" Hurt laces Greyson's voice.

"Of course I do. I love you, Greyson, but why can't I decide my own fate? Shouldn't I be allowed to tie myself to you by my own choice? You're making decisions for me and that makes me feel like I did when I was under my father's control." I know those words cut him deep, but they're what I feel and I won't lie to him to make him feel better.

"Now I'm controlling you like your father did. What the hell is wrong with you?" He throws his glass into the fireplace and whirls to glare at me. "I thought you loved me, but I guess you were just using me to get away from your father."

He stalks to the study door. I want to apologize, but I can't. As his hand touches the doorknob, I move.

"Wait."

He stares at the door, but doesn't look at me. I place my palm between his shoulder blades. The tension in his muscles makes me wonder if he's angry or fearful. I let my hand slide around to rest over his heart as I lean my forehead against his back.

"You do control me." I feel him stiffen. "But unlike my father, you control me with love and the desire to protect me, even while you're leading me into danger. Now you're afraid I'll let you leave without me. You're afraid that your love isn't enough for me to leave my country and risk my life." I pause.

After a moment, he nods.

"I never said I wouldn't go. I just asked to be allowed to make the choice for myself. You've been telling me from the moment I met you that you would never make my decisions for me." I force him to turn around and meet my eyes. "I only want to be asked, not told what I'm going to do."

He stares at me and I try to show how much I love him in my eyes. A slight smile breaks over his face. Cupping my chin in his hands, he brushes a kiss over my mouth.

"Will you come with me, Angel? I'd probably be worthless if you don't. Always worried about you and what you're doing. If you don't want to come, I'll leave this house open and you can stay here or at any of my estates." His arms wrap around me and I lay my head on his chest.

I'm happy that he is willing to ask, even though now he knows what my answer will be. "I'll go. There's nowhere else I'd rather be than by your side, Greyson. I need to make sure you see me as an equal, or at least as equal as I can be."

He whispers a kiss over my hair. "I'll try to remember to ask, but you might have to kick me once in a while."

I bring our lips together in a gentle kiss. A promise between the two of us to never take the other for granted. Before we can take it farther, a knock sounds on the door.

"Your grace, we need to talk to you about the servants and Mr. Roberts is here," the butler calls through the door.

"We need to be in Dover as soon as we can. Let's go have an adventure, Angel." Greyson smiles at me as he opens the door.

I'm not sure I need to start a new adventure when I haven't finished the one I started all those weeks ago.

Part Four

I'm watching the dockworkers carry our trunks onto Greyson's yacht. I admit to feeling a certain excitement. I long to be away from England for a while. Too many bad memories are left in my mind. Maybe the time away will ease them and I can start replacing them with good ones.

In Paris, I won't be the awkward laughingstock I have been here in my own country. I'll be the heir to one of the oldest Earldoms in England, plus the close personal friend of the Duke of Northampton. No one will ever need to know just how close we are. Though I assume there will be rumors flying within moments of our arrival in Paris, but for the first time, the thought of the gossip doesn't bother me.

It doesn't matter if Parisian society accepts me or not. I've already gone through the worst a person can deal with. Being ostracized by nobles will be a mere irritation, not a life-ending occasion. I'm not going there to make friends. I'm going to help my lover spy.

After we made love the night before, Greyson explained to me what the Home Office fears Napoleon's ambitions are. A chill creeps down my spine when I think about them. I'm not sure if I'll be able to actually help the duke, but I'm willing to try.

I feel a touch on my sleeve. I smile as I turn, expecting to see Greyson standing next to me. He said he would join me down at the docks when he finished meeting with the man the Home Office had sent. Surprise runs through me when I see a tall handsome young man there instead.

His blond hair is bleached almost white. His skin tanned a light brown. The clothes he wears are of a poorer quality than mine and though it looks like he tries to take care of them, there are smudges of dirt on them. He seems to be down on his luck. I reach into my pocket for some coins. I'm willing to help out someone in need.

"Sir, are you Angel?" His accent is a little rough, but his tone is polite.

I step back. He knows my name. Is this a trap by my father to keep me from leaving? I tug the coins out of my pocket and hold them out to him.

"I'll give you some coins, but I suggest you leave me alone now." I'm proud that my voice doesn't shake.

He shakes his head and steps back from my hand. "Thank you, sir, but I'm not asking for money. Do you know a man named Shade?"

At the mention of that name, I straighten up and lean forward. "What about Shade? Is he in trouble?"

Again he shakes his head. "No sir. He is offering to help my family and me out, but I don't know if I can trust him. He says to come and find you. He describes you and tells me to ask you about him."

Relief floods me. "I know him and you can trust Shade. He wouldn't hurt you unless you tried to hurt him first."

"Well, my little brother tried to pick his pocket earlier. Mr. Shade followed him to where we're staying. I was afraid he'd try to turn us into the constable. He says he has some work for us, but I'm not sure. He doesn't look like gentry." The young man seems puzzled.

Laughing, I gesture for him to follow me to a tavern just off the docks. I order us ale and lean against the building, keeping an eye on the loading process. "He isn't gentry, but he has connections in the landed class. If he says he has a job for you, I'm sure he'll have one."

"Why would he do this?"

I shrug and sip my ale. "No one really knows why Shade does what he does. Just accept it."

The man finishes his ale and sets the tankard down. Nodding to me, he starts to leave.

"Wait." He looks at me. "When you see Shade, tell him to go

to the earl. My uncle will help you all."

Fear fills his eyes. "I'm sorry, my lord. I didn't know you were related to an earl." He's worried, I can tell by the way he twists his hands together.

"Don't worry. There is no way you could have known. Shade wasn't trying to get you in trouble. He's a friend and if he wants to help you, than I want to as well. Just make sure you tell him to see my uncle." I grab his hand and drop the coins in his hand. "You weren't asking for them, but I want to give them to you. Get something for your family to eat."

He looks at the pile of gold coins in his hand before he looks up at me. A hint of pride shines in his eyes.

"Just take them. Don't let pride get in the way of a good meal," I say, knowing he's contemplating giving the money back.

"Yes, my lord." He touches his cap and bows slightly.

I smile as he walks away.

"Who was that?" Greyson arrives at my side as the young man disappears around the corner.

"Just someone asking for directions." I didn't feel the need to explain to the duke. "They're just finishing up loading the trunks. Are you sure we need to take all this stuff? And why are we taking your boat when we could just take the ferry?"

Greyson snorts. "No self-respecting duke would be caught dead on the ferry. No matter how silly and inconvenient it is, one must use all the toys his wealth and position affords him."

"Hmm." I don't response to his nonsense.

"Are you ready to leave England, love?" he asks softly after he makes sure no one is standing close enough to hear us.

I think about it for a minute or two. Finally, I nod. "Yes, I believe I am."

His hand caresses my buttocks and then he's heading to the yacht. I chuckle and follow.

Part Five

I stand on the deck of Greyson's yacht, watching the coast of England move away from me. At one time I would have been terrified at the thought of traveling anywhere beyond the borders of my country.

Greyson's love has taught me courage and proven to me that I'm strong. I could survive without him, but I chose not to. One of his arms encircles my waist and I lean against him with a sigh.

"What are you thinking?" His voice dances in my ear.

I rub my own hand over his hip. We moan. His hand slips down to rest lightly over my shaft. My hand covers his and presses his palm tighter to me. I want to feel his skin on mine. I'm glad that the railing hides what we're doing from prying eyes.

"We can't do anything here. There are still people watching from the dock."

Opening my eyes, I look at the dock we'd just left. He's right. A crowd gathers, since it isn't every day a duke departs on a voyage. I grin to myself. They all think we're running away from a scandal, though not many of them know what type of gossip would be following us. No one knows we're leaving on a mission for the government.

A movement among the crowd catches my eye. I study the faces. A pair of light green eyes catches my gaze. I start to point Shade out to my love, but an instinct tells me Shade is here to say goodbye to me. I raise my hand and smile. Returning the gesture, Shade bows his head slightly. I know he's also saying goodbye to a long dead lover who has haunted him for thirteen years. A hint of sadness fills my heart. I find myself hoping he finds someone to give him back his heart. A heart my cousin and my uncle broke all those years ago. Will I ever meet the man again? I hope so.

A man moves next to Shade and I realize it's the young man who questioned me a while ago. He waves to me and I nod back.

I hope Shade takes my advice and goes to my uncle. It's a way to bring them together and also help the young man's family.

I close my eyes again and snuggle closer to the duke. I reach behind him to stroke a hand over his ass. His groan causes a surge of pride to rush through me. I'm the only one who can make him lose his fabled control. Who would have imagined that an unassuming man like me would be able to hold the heart of a duke in his hands? I never thought I'd have a life full of love or a man who'll love me no matter what.

"I'm happy we're leaving," I murmur as I lay my head on his shoulder and give him access to more of my neck. We're far enough away from the dock that the watchers wouldn't be able to see us clearly.

"For a little while. We'll be back when we've got the information we need." Greyson presses a kiss to my neck. I shiver as he scrapes his teeth over my skin and finds the tender spot beneath my ear.

Of course we'll be back. His estates can't be left overlong to the care of managers, no matter how competent those men are. Also, we have to come back to reestablish his relationship with his sons. I don't want them to go through life thinking their father doesn't love them, not when I can see how much Greyson does care for them. There is still time to save their family. I must return to learn how to manage my uncle's estates as well. England is our home. All the pain and hurt I've suffered here doesn't change that fact. I'll miss so many things about my country, but it'll be interesting to get away.

I laugh softly. "I never imagined my life would turn out this way."

When we are far enough away from the docks, he turns me to face him, bracing his arms on the railing to either side of me. The Channel breeze teases his hair. My fingers itch to play with those golden locks. Leaning in, he takes a quick kiss. "Like what?"

"Happy. Who knew the pathetic creature I used to be would ever be loved by a god like you?" I chuckle as Greyson growls his displeasure. He hates when I talk about myself like this. "And that I'd ever learn to love someone like I love you."

"Hmm." Greyson hums as he takes my mouth with single-mindedpurpose. My lover is no longer interested in talking.

Wrapping my arms around his neck, I yield to him. His hands cup my ass and rock me against him. He slips a hand under my shirt, caressing the small of my back. I no longer cringe at the thought of him touching my scars. Greyson has taught me the beauty in my wounds. He says they are the marks of my courage. I'm not sure I believe that, but they do not repulse me anymore. I embrace the old and new ones as symbols of broken chains and new life.

"Let's go to our cabin, love," he demands.

I am his love. He shows me every day in a thousand different ways how much he loves me. I don't need to hear the words. I wouldn't believe them if he did say them to me often. Words can be easily said and lies roll off tongues with speed. Yet a simple touch to my hand and a soft smile on his face tells me more than any four-letter word could. He knows my love is just as strong. I take the hand he offers me.

I'm willing. As we walk to the stairs leading down into the yacht, I glance back one last time. The coast is a faint black line on the horizon. When I return to our home, it'll be different. I'll be different.

"Angel." Greyson's voice lures me away from the past.

I smile up into the blue gaze I adore. He is my piece of paradise. I'm like a fallen angel returning to the place I've always longed to be. I step into Greyson's arms and sigh. Peace, love and happiness. These emotions well in me and I find them reflected in my lover's eyes.

I've spent my time in Hell. Now it's time to forever embrace Heaven.

About the Author

There is beauty in every kind of love, so why not live a life without boundaries? Experiencing everything the world offers fascinates me and writing about the things that make each of us unique is how I share those insights. When not writing, I'm watching movies, reading and living life to the fullest.

Find TA on the internet at: http://www.tachase.com

Rainbow Romance Writers

Raising the Bar for LGBT Romance

RRW offers support and advocacy to career-focused authors, expanding the horizons of romance. Changing minds, one heart at a time. www.rainbowromancewriters.com

The Trevor Project

The Trevor Project operates the only nationwide, around-the-clock crisis and suicide prevention helpline for lesbian, gay, bisexual, transgender and questioning youth. Every day, The Trevor Project saves lives though its free and confidential helpline, its website and its educational services. If you or a friend are feeling lost, alone, confused or in crisis, please call The Trevor Helpline. You'll be able to speak confidentially with a trained counselor 24/7.

The Trevor Helpline: 866-488-7386

On the Web: http://www.thetrevorproject.org/

The Gay Men's Domestic Violence Project

Founded in 1994, The Gay Men's Domestic Violence Project is a grassroots, non-profit organization founded by a gay male survivor of domestic violence and developed through the strength, contributions and participation of the community. The Gay Men's Domestic Violence Project supports victims and survivors through education, advocacy and direct services. Understanding that the serious public health issue of domestic violence is not gender specific, we serve men in relationships with men, regardless of how they identify, and stand ready to assist them in navigating through abusive relationships.

GMDVP Helpline: 800.832.1901

On the Web: http://gmdvp.org/

Let us tell you a story.
A REALLY good story.
WARRIOR PRINCE
J.P. BOWIE
ISBN# 978-1-934531-88-4
BEND IN THE ROAD
Jeanne Barrack
ISBN# 978-1-608200-02-3
MLRPress.com
AVAILABLE ONLINE, AT LOCAL BOOKSTORES & THRU INGRAM

If you're a GLBT and questioning student heading off to university, you should know that there are resources on campus for you. Here's just a sample:

GLBT Scholarship Resources
http://www.hrc.org/resources/entry/tell-us-about-an-lgbt-scholarship

Syracuse University
http://lgbt.syr.edu/

Texas A&M
http://glbt.tamu.edu/

Tulane University
http://tulane.edu/studentaffairs/oma/lgbt/index.cfm

University of Alaska
http://www.uaf.edu/woodcenter/leadership/organizations/active/index.xml?id=61

University of California, Davis
http://lgbtrc.ucdavis.edu/

University of California, San Francisco
http://lgbt.ucsf.edu/

University of Colorado
http://www.colorado.edu/GLBTQRC/

University of Florida
http://www.multicultural.ufl.edu/lgbt/

University of Hawaii, Mānoa
http://manoa.hawaii.edu/lgbt/

University of Utah
http://www.sa.utah.edu/lgbt/

University of Virginia
http://www.virginia.edu/deanofstudents/lgbt/

Vanderbilt University
http://www.vanderbilt.edu/lgbtqi/